SECRET ADMIRER

After reading Penny's personal ad, Elizabeth burst out laughing. "Penny, this is hysterical. But you're not really going to use it, are you?"

"Why not?" Penny responded. "You see, I'm not totally convinced about this, but if I'm going to do it at all, I want my ad to be different. All the personal ads I've ever read sound more or less the same." She shrugged. "I'll probably get some pretty flaky answers, but I'm willing to sort through them."

"Are you sure you want to say this?" Enid said cautiously. "I mean, I hope you know what you're doing."

"Not necessarily," Penny said. "But when I see what kind of response *this* draws, I'll know whether there are really any boys around here with some imagination. Then we'll see. . . ."

Bantam Books in the Sweet Valley High Series
Ask your bookseller for the books you have missed

SWEET VALLEY HIGH

SECRET ADMIRER

Written by
Kate William

Created by
FRANCINE PASCAL

BANTAM BOOKS
TORONTO • NEW YORK • LONDON • SYDNEY • AUCKLAND

RL 6, IL age 12 and up

SECRET ADMIRER
A Bantam Book / September 1987
5 printings through June 1988

Sweet Valley High® is a trademark of Francine Pascal.

Conceived by Francine Pascal.

Produced by Cloverdale Press Inc.
133 Fifth Avenue, New York, N.Y. 10003.

Cover art by James Mathewuse.

ISBN 0-553-27691-3

Published simultaneously in the United States and Canada

Bantam Books are published by Bantam Books, a division of Bantam Doubleday
Dell Publishing Group, Inc. Its trademark, consisting of the words "Bantam
Books" and the portrayal of a rooster, is Registered in U.S. Patent and
Trademark Office and in other countries. Marca Registrada. Bantam Books,
666 Fifth Avenue, New York, New York 10103.

PRINTED IN THE UNITED STATES OF AMERICA

O   14   13   12   11   10   9   8   7   6   5

SECRET ADMIRER

One

It was Wednesday afternoon, and Elizabeth Wakefield couldn't think of a thing to write about. She tugged on a lock of sun-streaked blond hair and frowned at the blank sheet of paper in her typewriter.

"Writer's block, right?"

Looking up with a rueful smile, Elizabeth met Penny Ayala's steady, amused gaze. "Did you ever get the creepy feeling that you've forgotten your own language?" she asked.

Penny chuckled. "Sometimes I get so worked up I forget how to spell my own name." She pushed herself away from her desk and walked across the comfortable, cluttered space that was home to *The Oracle*, Sweet Valley High's student newspaper. "But I can't believe there isn't a single item for 'Eyes and Ears,' Liz, not in this hotbed of gossip. Isn't Jessica doing anything worth writing about?"

Repressing a grin, Elizabeth shook her head, but the twinkle in her blue-green eyes said the opposite. Wherever the action was, there was Elizabeth's twin, Jessica. And if there wasn't any action, then Jessica was sure to start some. So when it came to material for her weekly gossip column, Elizabeth was seldom at a loss.

"Actually, she's been suspiciously quiet these days," Elizabeth said, resting her chin in her hands. "But any day now something ought to pop up."

She lapsed into silence, still racking her brain for something to write about.

The column was supposed to be anonymously written, but Elizabeth's identity had long since become known, and "Eyes and Ears" was a popular feature of the paper. The gossip was never malicious or insinuating: Her column was always funny, and fun to read.

Penny ran a hand quickly through her short, dark blond hair. It was a gesture she used whenever she was deep in thought. As editor-in-chief of Sweet Valley High's newspaper, she had plenty of decisions to make, and lots of them were pretty tough, such as when to come down on one of her reporters for sloppy work or when to bump a story to make room for late-breaking news.

But Penny did manage to keep *The Oracle*—

and its busy staff—on a steady course without hurting anyone's feelings, a fact that had long since won her the respect of everyone who worked with her. And on top of that, she was one of the best students in the senior class.

Penny's ultimate goal was the same as Elizabeth's, as the girls had discovered long ago: to be a writer. She had wit, style, and imagination that showed up even in the smallest piece of work. She could write anything from hilarious parodies to sincere and moving poems. She and Elizabeth had shared many conversations about literature and writing, and spent long hours at the newspaper office together working on the paper.

"Let's see," she murmured, staring off into space. She met Elizabeth's gaze and gave her a lopsided grin. "I really shouldn't be doing your work for you, you know. One more slipup and you're out."

"What?" It was all Elizabeth needed to set her mind working, and she began tapping out her column on the typewriter, her jumbled thoughts suddenly organizing themselves.

Julie Porter gave a piano recital on Sunday at the Freundlich Gallery in Santa Monica, while The Droids played a gig at The Hot Potato on Saturday night. Lead singer Dana Larson belted out their new song, 'Put on Your Dancing Shoes' to a very receptive audience. Roger Patman placed second in Palisades' *Run for Kids* charity marathon on Tuesday afternoon. Cheering him on were Olivia Davidson, Bruce Patman, and Regina Morrow. . . .

"See how much you can remember when you need to?" Penny chuckled.

"Boy," Elizabeth grumbled. "If anyone knew what a slave driver you are, they'd never sign up for this dumb old newspaper."

The girls looked up quickly at the sound of a discreet cough from the doorway. "Hi, Liz, what's up?"

"Jessica!" Elizabeth saw the quizzical look in her twin's eyes and knew instantly what Jessica was thinking. To Jessica Wakefield, sitting in an office writing for a newspaper was just about as dull as you could get. She frequently pointed out all the exciting things Elizabeth could be doing besides writing for *The Oracle*. So the snippet of mock complaining Jessica had just overheard must have sounded serious enough to make her optimistic that her sister would be quitting the paper.

Penny turned away to hide a knowing grin, and Elizabeth shook her head with exaggerated solemnity. "Sorry, Jess, it's not what you're thinking."

Jessica assumed an air of injured dignity. "I don't know what you're talking about, Liz.

just wanted to tell you A
going to the mall after che
she's driving me home, so
OK?"

"Sure. Don't forget it's you
dinner, though. Right?"

There was a moment's hesitatio
toyed with the zipper of her burgu
duffel. If there was any way to get
chore at home, Jessica was always sure
it. That was one of her specialties, and n
just one example of the differences between
two Wakefield girls.

On the outside they were identical. Both were
five feet six with perfect size-six figures. Hours
of jogging, swimming, and tennis had given
them both a healthy tan, and their hair was a
sun-kissed honey gold. They even wore identical gold lavalieres, presents from their parents
on the twins' sixteenth birthday. Only a few
people knew about the small mole on Elizabeth's right shoulder, or noticed that Elizabeth
wore a wristwatch. Of course, Jessica would
never wear a watch, because time was completely meaningless to her. After all, it was her
belief that nothing ever got started until she
arrived anyway, so what did it matter what
time it was? Aside from those tiny observable
differences, they looked like duplicates.

On the inside, however, the Wakefield twins
were as different as night and day. Elizabeth

...fore Jessica, which
...nce in the world.
...th's motto. Her
..., and the quiet
...oyfriend, Jef-
...nid Rollins,
...d depend-
...r her loy-
...f person
...p, sym-
...y smile.

..., was like a spark of
...ng, and sometimes dan-
...dn't see tying herself down to
...—or anyone. Her closet was full of
...es she bought on impulse and wore only
once, and the rest of her life was like that, too.

But in spite of their differences, Elizabeth and Jessica shared a special bond that only identical twins could understand. Each one could always sense when her twin was troubled or sad, and they knew each other better than anyone else ever would.

And at the moment Elizabeth knew perfectly well that her twin was trying to think of some way to get out of cooking dinner. Their mother, a successful interior designer, sometimes came home late, so the girls were responsible for many of the household chores; it was a responsibility that Jessica didn't exactly treasure.

[torn corner fragment:] my Sutton and I are / erleading, and then / don't wait for me, / turn to cook / n as Jessica / ndy nylon / out of a / to find / was / the

"Right?" Elizabeth repeated, a warning note in her voice.

"Of course, Liz. The only thing is," she added with an angelic smile, "I don't want to upset Mom if dinner isn't ready when she comes home, so if I'm just a *little* bit late, could you start it? Please?"

Elizabeth groaned and dropped her head down onto her typewriter. She knew she would say yes. The funny thing was, she could always see Jessica's manipulations coming, but she never held them against her twin; that was just the way Jessica was. "OK," she muttered.

"Great! See you later, Liz." Jessica disappeared through the door. Penny and Elizabeth heard her say, "Hey, sorry," then Lynne Henry came through the door, grappling with an armload of books.

"Lynne, hi."

With a sigh of relief, Lynne set down a big, bulging manila envelope, then pulled out a chair for herself. Her almond-shaped, gold-flecked eyes twinkled as she nodded at the overstuffed envelope. "The first installment."

Penny came forward eagerly. "You mean the personal ads?" She stopped herself as she was reaching to pull out one of the many slips cascading onto the desk. "Sorry," she said sheepishly.

It was an idea Lynne had come up with to liven up the paper: Students would place personal ads in *The Oracle*, just as people did in the local papers. And even though Lynne wasn't a regular staff member, Penny had asked her to coordinate the new feature. Lynne was a shy, quiet junior, who devoted most of her free time to writing songs and playing her guitar. But a trustworthy coordinator was absolutely necessary for this type of column, and Lynne had agreed to fill the position.

"I think I've come up with the best system," she said, pushing her light brown hair behind her shoulders and leaning forward on her elbows. "People have put their names on the ad forms, so I know who they are, but I'm assigning everyone a number—like a post office box number—and that's what other people will use to respond. Then I'll look up who gets what, and I'll send or give them to people. I'm also prepared, once other schools find out about this, to send the responses to those people, too."

Elizabeth gave a low whistle, "Talk about organized!" she said. "Is that all of them?"

Lynne wrinkled her nose. "I'll probably get more tomorrow and Friday." She looked back at her desk and rolled her eyes. "I sure hope this system works."

"Of course it will work," Penny reassured Lynne. "But it looks like you got a lot more than you bargained for."

Lynne nodded. "Actually, it isn't as bad as it

looks. I already read some of them, and I can tell there are a lot of joke ads—you know, people who aren't really serious. If there's room, I'll run some of them, but at first I'm just going to pick the ones that are serious."

"What do you mean 'joke ads'?" asked Elizabeth.

Lynne rested her head on one hand and poked a finger at the pile in front of her. "Such as, 'Gorgeous British rock star looking for fans. Beautiful girls: send pictures and all your dreams will come true.' "

"Give me a break!" Penny laughed and shook her head.

"Well, some of them are funny-but-serious," Lynne added. "So those will go in."

"I can't wait to read them," Elizabeth said.

Sitting back at her desk, Penny picked up her red pencil and began editing an article. "Thinking about checking some of them out?"

"Hardly!" Elizabeth smiled and shook her head as she watched Lynne stacking the forms in a pile. She had a prize in Jeffrey French, and she knew it: He was warm, caring, and excitingly handsome. No, she wasn't interested in "checking some of them out." "But how about you, Pen?"

As soon as the words were out, Elizabeth realized she had made a mistake. Penny blushed and the girl turned her face back to the article.

"Don't be silly, Liz. You know I'm not into parties and things like that."

Lynne looked up with a frown to meet Elizabeth's worried gaze: a note of tension had entered the air. For some reason Penny Ayala didn't date anyone, even on a casual basis. Elizabeth had often wondered about it but had put it down to Penny's busy academic and extracurricular schedule. But Penny's quick blush suggested that perhaps it wasn't entirely her choice.

Elizabeth cleared her throat. "You know—"

"And how are the best writers in Sweet Valley?" came a cheerful male voice.

The three girls looked up as Roger Collins entered the office. The handsome, strawberry-blond English teacher was one of Sweet Valley High's favorites because of his relaxed and friendly attitude. He was a demanding teacher but a fair one, and he gave his time generously as faculty adviser to the newspaper.

He set a bundle of galley proofs down on Penny's desk and looked around. "Something going on here?"

"Just talking," Penny said with an offhand shrug. "Thanks for picking these up," she added as she reached for the galleys.

"Sure, no problem. Say, Liz, I've got something for your column." Mr. Collins perched on the edge of a table and crossed his arms. "A certain English teacher who shall remain nameless at this time has been asked by the student council dance committee to act as chaperon for the upcoming Forties Night Swing Fling."

"That's great! Are you—is *he*—going to agree?" Elizabeth's eyes danced as she smiled up at him.

"That depends on whether a certain French teacher—who shall also remain nameless—would like to join him."

Mr. Collins could be talking about only one person, and all three girls knew who that was: Nora Dalton, the pretty young French teacher. The two were a popular couple at Sweet Valley High, and almost every girl at school alternated between fierce envy and vicarious romantic bliss when it came to Nora Dalton.

"And that reminds me," he went on as he jumped down. "I expect to see you ladies there. I plan on jitterbugging with all three of you."

Elizabeth and Lynne laughingly agreed, and Mr. Collins collected some books and left the office. Elizabeth and Jeffrey were already looking forward to the forties-style dance, even though it was still a few weeks away. And Lynne was undoubtedly going with her boyfriend, Guy Chesney, who played keyboards for Sweet Valley's most popular band, The Droids.

But Elizabeth did notice color tinging Penny's cheeks again as she bent studiously over the article with her red pencil. "Are you going to the dance, Penny?" Elizabeth asked softly.

11

With another casual shrug, Penny shook her head. "Oh, you know. I'm too busy to go to the dances, I guess. Besides," she added with a bright smile, "I'm not really the type boys like to go out with."

"What is *that* supposed to mean?" Elizabeth asked, incredulous. "You mean boys don't like smart, pretty girls with a great sense of humor?"

Penny smiled wryly. "Liz, you're too polite. You know I'm not all that pretty—I guess I don't bother that much with my appearance. It just isn't as important to me as it is to some people."

"Yeah, like Jessica," Elizabeth said and chuckled, thinking of the hours her twin spent in front of the mirror. But it was true: Penny Ayala had a pretty face and was tall and thin, but she didn't take pains with her appearance. She was always dressed neatly. But she didn't use any makeup or wear flattering styles.

And on top of that, Elizabeth knew Penny was shy in a way that came across as aloofness. When you put it all together, Penny wasn't giving herself much of a chance. But Elizabeth thought it was too bad that most boys needed to be impressed by a girl's appearance before they could make an effort to see her inner qualities.

"Look, what do you two say if we finish this up and get some ice cream at Casey's Place before we go home?" Elizabeth asked.

Lynne smiled ruefully. "Sorry, I'm meeting

Guy after he finishes practicing with the band. But you two go ahead. I'll stay here a while longer and try to make some sense out of these ads."

"Penny?"

Penny looked down at the stack of papers on her desk and frowned. But then she met Elizabeth's gaze and smile. "Sure, why not?"

"That's the spirit!" Elizabeth typed the final period on her column and picked up her books. "Let's go."

As they left the school for the parking lot, Elizabeth sneaked a look at Penny. Was it her imagination, or had she detected a note of wistfulness behind Penny's nonchalance about dating?

"Penny, you can kill me if this is insulting, but you should learn how to lighten up a little around guys. Give them a chance to see how much fun you are."

Penny's face was impassive, and Elizabeth felt like kicking herself. She stopped and put her hand on Penny's arm. "I'm sorry."

For a moment Penny didn't speak. Her hazel eyes were clouded, as if she were looking at something far away. Then her face brightened in a warm smile. "Liz, I'm not mad at you. Hey, I know it's my own fault I turn boys off. They just don't like serious students, I guess. And frankly, I just can't see pretending to be something I'm not just to snag one."

She continued walking, and reached the red Fiat convertible that Elizabeth shared with her sister. "This is your car, right?"

Obviously Penny didn't want to talk about dating anymore, and Elizabeth felt she should respect her friend's feelings. But as they got in the car and headed downtown, Elizabeth couldn't help feeling that Penny was hiding a little bit of loneliness inside. And she wished there was something she could do to help.

Two

"I don't think I like this color after all." Lila Fowler looked down at the sleek, fire-engine-red maillot bathing suit she was wearing, then resettled herself on her beach blanket. "I mean, don't you think it kind of bleaches out my tan?"

Jessica stopped rubbing cocoa butter onto her legs for a moment and looked at Lila's new suit with a critical eye. "Mmm. It does a little." She resisted a smile as Lila's expression soured. At least Jessica knew her white string bikini was about as flattering as could be.

The only problem was, it wasn't doing her the least bit of good.

She rolled over onto her stomach and stared dismally at the glittering Pacific Ocean. For perhaps the tenth time that afternoon, she complained, "There just aren't any decent guys around here, Lila."

A groan rose from Lila's beach blanket. "Tell me about it!"

Between the two of them, Jessica and Lila had dated nearly all of the "acceptable" boys in Sweet Valley High. Nevertheless, they constantly bemoaned the shortage of new prospects.

"Hey," Lila said. "Do you know anything about that new guy—Kirk Anderson? He's pretty hot-looking."

"Yeah, well, that's about all he's got going for him," Jessica replied. "His personality rates a zero."

Jessica felt a rush of indignation as she remembered meeting Kirk. He was trying out for the varsity tennis team, and she had watched him appreciatively. With his jet-black hair, athletic build, and striking blue eyes, he had definitely looked like someone she might be interested in. But when he came over and looked her up and down so coolly and then had the gall to say she might get *lucky* some day, she had turned around and stalked away. That sort of superior attitude didn't cut it with her.

The gloomy silence descended again, and Jessica propped herself up on her elbows to look around. The beach was pretty crowded for a Thursday afternoon, and there were lots of her classmates around. Bill Chase and Ken Matthews were waxing their surfboards; cheerleaders Jean West and Sandra Bacon were also there working on their tans, as all of the cheerleaders did when there wasn't practice. Jean's boyfriend, Tom McKay, was sitting with them. Jessica noticed her sister sitting with Enid Rollins, a girl Jessica thought was about as exciting as a hot-water bottle. The same old Sweet Valley High crowd, Jessica thought with a sigh. If only there were some way to meet new boys!

As she looked around at the boys she knew, playing volleyball, throwing Frisbees, listening to radios, she decided they were all just too immature for her. In her opinion she was too sophisticated to date high school students. She had dated a few older boys—some without her parents' knowledge. And even though some of them had turned out to be real disasters, someone in college was what she wanted. But how to meet him?

"Lila, we've got to take some serious action," she declared, sitting upright. "There's got to be some way to meet some guys. *Older* guys."

Lila opened one eye and regarded her skeptically. They'd had this conversation dozens of times before without getting anywhere. "Oh, yeah? Like what?"

"Well . . ." Jessica knew if she voiced the idea that had been fermenting in her mind for the past week, Lila would probably throw a fit. But Lila was always throwing fits, so what difference would one more make? "I think we should use the personal ads in the *The Oracle*."

"What! That is the grossest idea you've ever

had, Jessica Wakefield!" Lila's voice was dripping with scorn, and she sat up to give her friend a withering glance. "Only losers take out personal ads, and only losers answer them."

Jessica rolled her blue-green eyes. "For your information, *Lila*, personal ads are not what they used to be. I read this article in *Ingenue* that said more and more singles use them to meet people because of the pressures of life these days. Lots of people don't have time to go cruising around, you know, so they just take out an ad to say exactly what they're looking for and then pick out the best replies."

Lila maintained a stony silence.

"It's *the* best way to meet people now," Jessica went on confidently. "They had these testimonials and pictures of couples who had met through the ads, and believe me, these people were not losers."

"Well, if you're so smart, how do you expect to meet college boys with ads in a high school paper?"

Jessica gave Lila a satisfied smile. "I just happen to know someone in college who gets copies of our paper, and that someone always has tons of good-looking friends in his room."

Of course, Lila would know she was talking about Steven, the twins' eighteen-year-old brother, who was a freshman at the state university. Steven faithfully read *The Oracle*, partly to keep up with Sweet Valley High news but mostly because of Elizabeth's articles.

A thoughtful look crossed Lila's face as she surveyed the beach. Jessica caught the expression and knew she'd won the first important round. She had to get Lila to do it with her—it was always more fun to do something like this with a friend.

"And you can always *say* that only college boys should reply," she continued pointedly. "You can spell out exactly what kind of guy you want, you know. Just list the requirements, and you'll get good-looking guys falling all over themselves to get to you."

Lila sniffed. "I would think it's a better idea to describe yourself. You know, tell them exactly what kind of person you are, and then the perfect guy who's been searching for you all his life will turn up."

"No way! You should describe what *you* want."

Scowling, Lila turned on her. "Oh, yeah? What makes you such a know-it-all, Jessica? Just because you read some stupid article doesn't make you an expert."

Jessica rummaged around in her pink duffel bag and pulled out a notebook. "Well, do it your way, and I'll do it my way—and we'll just see which way is best."

"A little competition, huh?" Lila said, beginning to smile.

"That's right! A contest—but not a bet, Lila."
Jessica frowned, thinking of all the bets she and
Lila had had. She was always confident, but
Lila had so much more money, since her father
was one of the richest men in Sweet Valley. So
it didn't make much difference to Lila if she
lost. But Jessica's financial resources were lim-
ited, and she'd be sunk if she lost a real bet.

"We'll each take out an ad and see what kind
of guys we get," she went on eagerly. "Then
we'll have some kind of double date, and we'll
each check out the other one and decide who
did better. We could all go to the Swing Fling
together or something."

Lila raised her eyebrows. "I *have* a date for
the Swing Fling," she said haughtily.

"Well, so do I," Jessica retorted. "But if you
found the man of your dreams, wouldn't you
rather go with him?"

"I guess so."

Jessica smiled with triumph. "OK. We'll each
write our ads and give them to Lynne Henry
tomorrow—that's the deadline." Without another word she handed her friend a sheet of
notebook paper and found an extra pencil. For
the next few minutes, the girls were silent, busy
composing their ads.

"You done?" Jessica said finally.

Lila frowned at her paper, then looked up
with a grin. "I think this ought to do it." She
handed her ad to Jessica.

20

Glamorous, sophisticated, mature high school girl looking for someone with the right stuff. I like fast cars, caviar, and the Caribbean. Don't talk to me about commitment—I'm looking for excitement, not a bridge partner. If you can keep up with me, I want you. *Kids need not reply.*

"Wow!" Jessica looked at Lila with appreciation. "You sure know how to write an ad. But I think you're approaching it from the wrong angle. Look at this."

Are you devastatingly handsome? Are you romantic and wild? Do you like girls who aren't afraid of danger? Are you the type of guy who goes for what he wants? Are you in college? If you answered yes to *all* the above questions, drop me a line. I've been looking for you.

Lila's eyes kindled with excitement. "This might just turn out to be the most interesting contest we've ever had, Jess."

"Lila, I think you might just be right."

"Enid, where did you meet this guy?" Elizabeth asked.

Enid Rollins carefully flicked a grain of sand

off her knee and met Elizabeth's look with a shy smile. "I told you, Liz. At that new bookstore downtown." She glanced over to where Jeffrey French and her date, Hugh Grayson, stood, knee-deep in the surf, talking with animated gestures. Then she met Elizabeth's dancing eyes again. "He's pretty nice, huh? Especially for someone from Big Mesa High."

"*Pretty* nice," Elizabeth teased, and gave Enid a playful shove that tipped her over on the sand. The two girls watched Jeffrey and Hugh for a moment longer. Coming from rival schools didn't seem to make any difference to the two boys. When their eyes met again, Elizabeth and Enid burst into laughter.

"Hey you two, no fighting on the beach! I'll call the police!" A gangly boy on a nearby beach blanket glared menacingly at them until the pretty, dark-eyed girl with him calmly threw a towel over his head.

"Maria!" His muffled voice was audible through the cloth. Elizabeth and Enid laughed even harder as Winston Egbert, the junior class's certified clown, staggered around, pretending to be under attack from the towel. "Help!" he yelled and collapsed onto the sand.

Winston and his girlfriend, Maria Santelli, were a popular couple. Maria was a vivacious, friendly girl on the cheerleading squad, always willing to help out on school projects. And Elizabeth remembered with admiration how Win-

22

ston had recently returned a winning lottery ticket that had accidentally come into his possession. Not many people would have owned up to it, but Winston had.

As Elizabeth looked around, shielding her eyes from the blazing afternoon sun, she caught sight of Penny Ayala standing across the sand from the parking lot. She waved, and Penny returned the wave, then veered in their direction.

"Hi, you guys," she said as she dropped to her knees in the sand. She hugged an armload of books and papers to her chest and cocked her head to one side. "Mind if I camp out here? I've got to get through this humongous pile."

"Sure," Enid said. They made a space for her on their beach blankets, and Penny began unpacking her gear.

Just then Jeffrey and Hugh walked up, still deep in conversation, and Penny's face fell.

"Penny, this is Hugh Grayson," Enid said, her pleasure obvious as she introduced the tall, pleasant-looking boy. He gave Penny a friendly smile and sat down next to Enid.

"Hey, Penny." Jeffrey picked up a towel and rubbed drops of salt water from his muscular arms. "Still hounding Liz, huh?"

Penny laughed but began picking up the books and papers she had just set down. "I'd be better off hounding myself, now that you mention it," she said lightly. She shrugged as she added,

"I think I really should sit by myself, or I'll never get anything done."

"Penny?" Elizabeth frowned as her friend stood up. "Are you sure you don't want to sit with us? We'll give you peace and quiet if that's what you need."

"Thanks, Liz. I really have too much work to do, and I know I'd never do it if I hung around here. I'll see you tomorrow, though. Besides, I don't want to be a fifth wheel."

Before they could protest, Penny turned and walked down the beach. Finding an isolated spot, she spread out her towel and sat down, then began poring intently over the papers in her lap.

The conversation bounced casually around Elizabeth as she gazed over at Penny. Her friend had seemed willing enough to sit with them before the boys came up. Penny and Jeffrey were friends, though, so Elizabeth knew Penny didn't leave because of any animosity. Was that quip about being a fifth wheel more serious than it sounded? Did Penny leave just because Elizabeth and Enid were there with dates?

The more Elizabeth pondered that question, the more convinced she became that that *was* the motive for Penny's sudden change of mind. And when she looked at the situation objectively, she couldn't blame her friend. It was always a slightly awkward situation to be in, even though it was ridiculous to feel that way.

If Penny had had a boy with her, she probably would have stayed, Elizabeth thought.

"You're looking pretty serious," Jeffrey murmured, pouring a thin trickle of sand onto Elizabeth's bare feet as he lay next to her. He looked up into her eyes, his own eyes filled with tenderness and concern. "Anything wrong?"

She couldn't help smiling at him. Even after months of dating, he could still make her heart do flip-flops when he looked at her that way. If there was one thing she could always count on with Jeffrey, it was that he always sensed when she had something on her mind.

"Not really," she said slowly. "Just someone I wish I could help, that's all."

He chuckled. "The usual."

If she spent a lot of time helping other people, Jeffrey didn't mind, or he at least understood, Elizabeth thought. In fact, sometimes it seemed as if he understood her almost better than she understood herself. Their friendship had started off as a mutual attraction, and quickly deepened into much more. That was one of the reasons she had recently decided to turn down a hard-won scholarship to a Swiss boarding school. She couldn't see letting go of a relationship as special as the one she shared with Jeffrey.

"Hey," she whispered, looking down thoughtfully into his eyes. "You're a pretty OK guy, you know?"

He snorted. Then his smile softened, and he

raised himself on one elbow to kiss her gently on the lips.

"Hey, you two," Enid teased, her curly hair tumbling into her eyes as she glanced over at them. "This is a public place, remember?"

"Hmm, I almost forgot," Jeffrey murmured, still looking intently at Elizabeth.

She laughed and, putting one hand on his arm, gave him a mischievous grin. "Listen, Jeffrey, how about taking Hugh over and introducing him to Ken and Bill, OK?"

"Are you trying to get rid of us?"

Hugh and Enid paused in their own conversation and looked over at them. Hugh raised his eyebrows in a humorously cynical expression. "Something tells me we're keeping these two from some important conversation."

Elizabeth laughed. "Well, if you don't *mind*," she said, pushing Jeffrey to his feet.

"OK! OK! We're going."

Enid rolled over onto her stomach and fixed Elizabeth with an expectant look once the boys were safely out of earshot. "Well?"

"Enid, listen. Did you notice how Penny wanted to leave when the guys showed up?" Enid nodded, and Elizabeth went on, her forehead creased in a thoughtful frown. "Well, I was talking to her yesterday, and I got the impression that she's really kind of lonely, but she doesn't know how to attract boys."

"You're kidding? But she's so funny and smart

and everything! She might even be valedictorian this year."

"I know. But she's really shy, Enid. She acts like she's so together, but I think she really feels left out sometimes."

Enid's gaze traveled across the sand to where Penny sat alone, and she nodded slowly. "I guess I see what you mean. She just takes off when there are guys around. I mean, she acts as if it doesn't matter, but you could be right. Well, what do you have in mind? Because I *know* you have something in mind, Elizabeth Wakefield!"

Biting her lower lip, Elizabeth looked at her best friend again. "Well, you're going to have to help me convince her. I want her to take out a personal ad in *The Oracle*."

"What? She'd *never* go for that, Liz. Not Penny."

"I know, but—" She broke off and nervously pleated the edge of her towel. "See, she's afraid that boys don't want to date her because she's so smart and such a serious student. As if she wouldn't be any fun at all. But my idea is that if she has some anonymous correspondence with a guy and he gets to know her personality, he'll *know* what a wonderful girl she is, and all that other stuff won't matter. See?"

Enid nodded again. "You've got a point there. I guess that's what appeals to people about personal ads to begin with."

"That's right," Elizabeth added quickly. "And she doesn't think she's at all attractive, either, which is just ridiculous. But don't you think that'll make her like the idea even more?"

Enid fingered a curl and shrugged, "I don't know, Liz. Something tells me she's going to say no."

"Well, that's why we have to convince her, you dope." Elizabeth stood up and grabbed Enid's hand. "Come on. There's no time like the present."

They jogged quickly over the sand to Penny, who looked up in surprise as they plopped down beside her.

"Hi." Her voice held a note of wary hesitation, as though she suspected they were up to something.

"Listen, Penny. I've got this great idea, and I don't want you to say a thing till I've told you all about it."

"Sounds pretty drastic, Liz." Penny smiled, "OK, what is it?"

Penny listened in silence as Elizabeth and Enid gave her all the good reasons why she should use a personal ad to meet someone. But when they were finished, she gave them a wistful smile and shook her head.

"I don't know. It seems—"

"Penny, come on," Elizabeth pleaded. "What can it hurt? If none of the answers you get appeal to you, then you can drop the whole thing, and no one will have any idea you were involved. Just try it, OK?"

A group of girls ran past them, shrieking with mock fear as their boyfriends chased them with buckets of water. Laughing, the whole gang plunged noisily into the surf. A flicker of sadness crossed Penny's face. Then, she seemed to come to a decision.

"OK," she said firmly. She met their serious expressions and laughed. "Come on, you two, don't look so grim. This could be fun. And," she added thoughtfully, "it might even work."

Elizabeth released a long sigh of relief. "Great. Do you want us to help you write the ad?"

With a little chuckle, Penny shook her head. "Listen, if there's one thing I do have plenty of confidence about, it's writing. But will you both look at it when I'm done and see how it reads?" Her smile was poignantly hopeful as she looked from Elizabeth to Enid.

They nodded vigorously and sat back while she put her pencil to her lips. Finally she gave a quick nod, bent over her notebook, and began writing. A faint smile showed at the corners of her mouth. "I'm not giving it to Lynne until after the first issue comes out, though. I want to wait and see what kind of reaction the school has to the new feature."

She circled the paragraph emphatically, then handed to to Elizabeth. Enid read over her shoulder:

Hook-nosed hunchback seeks kindred spirit. The ideal candidate will have a doctorate in Australian theology, love caves, speak Urdu. If you're looking for a girl who giggles, don't bother to respond. I'm strictly the guffaw type. Junior or senior will do just fine.

Elizabeth burst out laughing. "Penny, this is hysterical. But you're not really going to use it, are you?"

"Why not?" Penny responded, "You see, I'm not totally convinced about this, but if I'm going to do it at all, I want my ad to be different. All the personal ads I've ever read all sound more or less the same." She shrugged. "I'll probably get some pretty flaky answers, but I'm willing to sort through them."

"Are you sure you want to say this?" Enid said cautiously. "I mean, I hope you know what you're doing."

Penny gave them a rueful smile. "Not necessarily. But when I see what kind of response *this* draws, I'll know whether there are really any boys around here with some imagination. Then we'll see."

She glanced down at the ad she had just composed and repeated softly, "We'll see."

Three

On the following Monday, the first issue of *The Oracle* running personal ads came out. The new feature created an unprecedented sensation at Sweet Valley High: Even by Friday the paper was still in evidence all over the school. In the cafeteria, out on the sprawling front lawn, and in the hallways, students were seen bent over the new personal ads with unmistakable excitement.

And when the second issue rolled off *The Oracle*'s press, there was a mad rush to get copies as soon as possible. That Monday afternoon Jessica and Amy Sutton passed by the tennis courts on their way to cheerleading practice. A gang of boys from the team was sitting on the grass, reading personal ads out loud amid raucous laughter and joking.

"Don't you think those ads are a riot?" Amy

asked, sending a brief, but unnoticed smile over toward the boys. Years ago Amy had been a good friend of Elizabeth's, and somewhat of a tomboy. Then she and her family had moved East, and Jessica had thought it was good riddance. Unexpectedly, the Suttons had moved back to Sweet Valley, and the sixteen-year-old Amy was as boy-crazy as Jessica was, much to Elizabeth's disappointment. Now Amy was much better friends with Jessica and Lila than with Elizabeth.

Well, at least I don't have to worry about those clowns answering my ad, Jessica congratulated herself silently. Out loud she added, "Yeah, what a joke. Hang on a minute."

Pausing for a moment to retie the laces of her sneakers, she looked speculatively at the noisy huddle. At the center of the action was the new boy, Kirk Anderson. He was obviously used to being the ringleader of whatever group he was in. His voice carried above all the others as he called imperiously for silence.

"Listen to this one guys: 'Hook-nosed hunchback seeks kindred spirit!' "

Jessica's lip curled, and she stood up again. *How immature*, she said to herself derisively. "Let's go, Amy."

"Say, Jess." Amy giggled. "Don't you think that guy Kirk is cute?"

"Forget it. He's the most arrogant and conceited guy in California."

She looked back over her shoulder for a moment, caught a glimpse of Neil Freemount sitting in Kirk's orbit, and felt a twinge of surprise. She and Neil had gone out a number of times: He was a very nice-looking guy, and a formidable opponent on the tennis court, two qualities Jessica liked a lot in her dates. But he had always remained more of a friend than a boyfriend.

But she had sensed a serious side to Neil, too, a side that sometimes seemed to disapprove of her carefree habits. He didn't seem like the kind of guy to be hanging around Kirk Anderson, she thought. Neil had been the one who introduced Jessica to Kirk, but she had assumed they just knew each other from the tennis team.

She shrugged and put the entire category of high school boys out of her mind. Sooner or later guys would start answering *her* ad!

Amy chuckled suddenly, breaking into Jessica's thoughts. "Well, I wasn't really interested in Kirk anyway. Can you keep a secret?"

"Of course I can, Amy," Jessica retorted. If it was a secret worth keeping, she thought.

With a conspiratorial grin, Amy lowered her voice. "Actually, I think there might be something between Bruce and me."

Jessica stared. "Bruce *Patman*? Amy, your brain has turned to mush. He's crazy about Regina Morrow, and you know it."

Amy just looked smug. "Well, we're working on this documentary together in our minicourse on films, and I have a feeling we're going to be spending a lot of time together. A *lot* of time," she repeated with a coy smile.

"Amy, forget it!" Jessica laughed airily and swung her duffel over one shoulder. "If there's one couple around here that's solid, it's Bruce and Regina."

"Maybe you're right," Amy said sweetly. "But we'll just see."

On Tuesday afternoon Elizabeth, Lynne, and Penny were in the newspaper office again. Neither Elizabeth nor Penny could disguise their curiosity over the pile of sealed letters on Lynne's desk.

For a few minutes Lynne shuffled papers with a look of intense concentration, but she finally looked up and caught them both staring at her.

"I feel like I'm about to be pounced on," she said wryly.

Penny felt her face burning as she made a flustered reply. She sent Elizabeth a guilty smile and got a warm nod of encouragement in return.

"I can't believe there are so many answers," Elizabeth said, shaking her head with amazement. "Who would have thought there'd be such a good response?"

Lynne bit her lip as she scanned her confidential list of "post office box numbers," and wrote a name on one envelope. "Can you believe that some of them are for yesterday's ads already?" she commented absently.

Penny's heart gave an unexpected leap. Would it be too much to hope there would be an answer to her crazy ad so soon?

Diligently turning back to her editorial work, Penny tried, without much success, to quell the growing surge of hope in her heart. The quiet rustling of papers was the only sound in the office for several interminable minutes.

Suddenly Lynne gasped, put a hand to her mouth, and looked at the other two girls with a stricken expression. "You know," she said uncomfortably, "I hope people aren't treating this as a joke." She shook her head, as if trying to dispel the unpleasant thought. "There are so many answers—I just hope they're all serious. Someone could really get hurt in a situation like this."

"Oh, Lynne, I don't think anybody would do that," Elizabeth said hastily.

"Well, I sure hope you're right. I never would have gotten involved in this if I thought anyone would take advantage of another person's vulnerability."

With a resigned sigh, Lynne continued sorting and addressing the letters. At one point she stood up and crossed the room to Elizabeth. "Your sister is doing all right," she said quietly, a lopsided smile lighting her amber-flecked eyes. "And her letters are coming through the regular U.S. mail." She placed a packet of letters in front of Elizabeth, and added in a low voice, "I wouldn't do this with anyone else, but since you're her sister, I figured it would be OK— isn't it? I know I can trust you."

"Sure, Lynne. I'm sure Jess won't mind. She'll just be glad she got hers early. Thanks."

Penny raised her eyebrows. She never would have thought pretty, popular Jessica Wakefield, a girl who was never without a date, would resort to placing a personal ad. It suddenly made her chances seem even better. After all, if girls like Jessica were placing ads, wasn't it just as likely that really special guys would answer them?

"Uh, Penny?"

She hardly dared raise her eyes to Lynne's face. When she did, it was to see Lynne holding three envelopes toward her. Penny took the sealed letters with an attempt at nonchalance. She set them on he desk and rested her arm on them without even glancing at them. But the paper beneath her elbow seemed to burn into her skin.

"Thanks." It was a hoarse whisper.

Lynne sighed. "All done. I'm going to take these to the main office so that people will get them tomorrow." She stood and gathered all the letters together and shrugged into her light jacket. "See you tomorrow."

When the door shut behind Lynne, there was an air of suspense in the little office.

"Well?" Elizabeth demanded finally, her face glowing with excitement. Their eyes met, and Elizabeth's cheeks colored slightly. "I'm sorry, Penny. I know you'd rather read them by yourself."

"No, no! Liz, I want you to stay and read them with me. Please?" Penny tried to make her voice sound casual, but she was painfully aware that Elizabeth knew her too well to be deceived. "I mean, this could be a lot of fun, right?"

Elizabeth smiled and gave her a quick nod. "Well, you read them first, and you can decide if you want me to see them."

That was all the prompting Penny needed. She hurriedly slit open the first letter with a pencil. Running her eye over the page, she quickly determined that "Mr. X," as he called himself, was not a likely candidate.

"Take a look at this," she said, handing over the letter.

"Are you really hook-nosed and hunchbacked," Elizabeth read, "or was that supposed to be a joke? I guess it must be a joke because there isn't anybody like that at Sweet Valley High. Anyway, you sound pretty smart, and maybe we could get together and you could help me with my homework."

Elizabeth laughed. "Oh, Penny! No wonder he needs help with his homework. He must be pretty dense if he had to ask if it was a joke."

"No kidding," Penny muttered, rolling her eyes. "So far we're off to a great start."

She opened the second letter and scanned it quickly. Then she groaned. "This one wants to get together so we can compare our auras." She laughed ruefully. "He took that part about kindred spirits a little too literally. He says he wants to see my astrological chart."

A look of utter astonishment settled on Elizabeth's face. "You're got to be kidding! I didn't know anyone actually believed in that stuff."

"Surprise, surprise." Penny drew a deep breath and looked at the last unopened letter in front of her. So far the results had been a crushing disappointment, and she felt a flutter in her chest as she opened the letter. If only it was *him*, the boy she'd been hoping for.

Dear Quasimodo:

Just got back from my latest cave-cleaning job and saw your ad. I think I've been hoping to find you ever since I graduated from the University of Western Australia. The outback was too quiet for me. You sound like the kind of girl I'd really like to meet.

But let me tell you about myself. I love to read, hike, speak Urdu—the usual things. I may not have a hook nose or a hunchback, but I'm told I'm reasonably good-looking in spite of it. I've managed to live with this infirmity all my life, and I've been looking for someone who might be able to overlook it. I get the distinct impression you could be that girl: smart, funny, but sensitive. Am I right?

I'm tired of girls who make superficial judgments at the beginning of a relationship. I know it takes time to really get to know someone.

If you write back, I'll be really happy.

Best wishes,
Jamie

Penny handed the letter to Elizabeth and watched breathlessly while her friend read Jamie's letter.

As she read, Elizabeth began to smile, and once she actually laughed out loud. "Penny, he's just as goofy as you are."

She nodded quickly. It was unbelievable, but whoever Jamie was, he had taken her quirky sense of humor in stride. And he obviously had a pretty quick mind too. He'd been able to read between the lines of her personal ad, something she hadn't even dared to hope for. Maybe it was too soon to tell, but she thought she and

Jamie could really hit it off. The only problem was, there was no one named Jamie at Sweet Valley High.

Elizabeth echoed her thoughts. "Jamie? I wonder who he is?"

"Well, it's probably an alias, don't you think? He doesn't want to give away his identity too soon."

There was a brief silence as the two girls reread the letter. Finally Elizabeth looked up and met Penny's eyes. "You've really got something here, Pen. He sounds like an interesting person. Are you going to write back?"

"Of course!" The possibility of letting Jamie get away was unbearable. "Only, could you and Enid help me do it?" She blushed and looked away. How could she admit to Elizabeth how hopeful and excited she was? And scared. Elizabeth's love life seemed so smooth and easy: she had a boyfriend who was crazy about her. How could Elizabeth begin to imagine what this letter meant to Penny?

But Elizabeth seemed to read her thoughts. She squeezed Penny's arm and said, "Sure. Let's go to my house, OK? I'll call Enid and tell her to meet us there."

"Thanks, Liz."

"Well, that should do it, don't you think?"

Elizabeth poured herself another glass of iced

tea and took the letter from Penny. As she sat back in the chaise longue, Enid leaned over her shoulder and read with her:

Dear Jamie:

I was sorry to hear about your deformity (the lack of h-n and h-b), but I guess I'm in no position to be picky.

Seriously, though, I like to read—almost anything, but especially the classics: Dickens, Alcott, Austen, you name it. (But I prefer them in the original Urdu.) The last book I read was *Lord of the Flies*, and I thought it was pretty incredible. Have you read it? I guess you could say I'm a pretty serious student, but I do like to have fun.

The beach is one of my favorite places, but I like to go when it's almost deserted—very early in the morning is my favorite time. I saw a school of whales once, and I'll never forget it.

I also like to write, and that's one reason I'm having so much fun right now. Something tells me you and I are pretty much alike, and I'll bet you collect those plastic rings from six-packs, just like I do. But could I have read you wrong? Please write back and set my mind at rest.

Yours truly,
Quasimodo

A late-afternoon shaft of sunlight slanted through the lemon trees in the Wakefields' back-yard and lit Penny's face. Elizabeth couldn't help smiling at her.

"I think it's fine, Penny. I think your personality really shows through, and I know he'll be able to tell what parts are serious and what parts aren't."

Penny nodded solemnly. "Yeah. I'd hate it if he thought the six-pack rings were a joke."

"Penny!" Enid scolded.

The three girls chuckled, and Penny folded the letter and slipped it inside a notebook. Then she glanced at her watch and gave them a rueful smile. "I think I'd better go home. It's almost dinnertime."

"Wouldn't you like to stay and have dinner here?" Elizabeth asked.

"Oh . . . no, no, thank you," Penny stammered, her shyness returning. "I'd better go."

Elizabeth walked with her out to the street and waved as Penny walked away down the sidewalk. Then she strolled back to the patio to rejoin Enid. She was about to comment on Penny's sense of humor, but the words died on her lips when she saw her friend's grave expression. "What's wrong?"

Enid was sitting at the edge of the pool. She looked up as Elizabeth sat down next to her.

"I just hope Penny doesn't end up getting hurt, Liz," Enid said softly.

Elizabeth felt a flicker of anxiety, but she tried to ignore it. "What do you mean?"

"Well, it's just that Penny's the type of person who expects a lot from a relationship. She thinks this Jamie guy is going to turn out to be everything she wants, and what if he isn't?"

Elizabeth knew that Enid had a valid point. Penny was obviously building her hopes up high: What if they ended up crashing down around her? Penny would have a really difficult time getting over a disappointment like that. And she might not ever try again. Penny was a very private person. It had taken a lot of courage to write that ad, Elizabeth knew, and if something went wrong. . . .

"Let's just hope it works out, Enid," was all Elizabeth could say.

Penny slowly lowered her copy of *The Scarlet Letter* to her lap and stared into space. There was no use trying. She just couldn't concentrate. The sealed letter propped up against her desk lamp kept drawing her attention. That letter, and what it represented, filled her with hope. If only it worked out!

Suddenly she couldn't sit still. She jumped up from her bed and began pacing around her room. Framed awards and merit certificates lined one whole wall of her small bedroom, and her bookshelves were overflowing with an eclectic assortment of novels and non-fiction books. Her electric typewriter, a Christmas gift from her parents, sat on one edge of the desk, and notebook after notebook of her own writing stood in neat rows beside her bed.

But now for the first time she began to wonder if all that was enough. Books and certificates were cold companions, and she had never felt more alone.

Her feverish pacing brought her to a halt in front of her mirror, and she studied her face with unusual attention. Her skin was clear, if a little pale, and her hair was cut straight and short. Her gaze traveled down to her clothes, and she frowned irritably. Why did she dress so unimaginatively? she wondered. Her beige corduroys, cotton blouse, and loafers were neat enough, but hardly made her look exciting or fashionable.

"How can you expect any guy to look at you when you're so boring?" she scolded her reflection. "Why don't you make more of an effort with yourself, you dope?"

With an impatient tug, Penny yanked open the top drawer of her bureau. Somewhere inside was a makeup sampler her aunt had given her a few months ago. She opened it up and looked skeptically at the eye shadows, blushers, and lip gloss.

With a little experimentation she could transform herself, she realized. If she put a little color on her cheeks and emphasized her eyes with mascara, she would look pretty nice. And she did have a good figure, so if she could find something more flattering . . .

She stared at herself again, biting nervously at her lower lip. If she was ever going to meet Jamie, she wanted him to be impressed. Because whoever he was, she didn't want to let him get away.

Four

As soon as dinner was over, Jessica pushed herself away from the table.

"I'm doing homework tonight with Lila," she announced. "Got to run."

Alice Wakefield put down her fork and regarded her daughter steadily. It was easy to see where the twins had gotten their good looks. Mrs. Wakefield was very pretty, and young enough to be mistaken occasionally for the girls' older sister.

"Isn't it your turn to do the dishes tonight, Jess?" Mrs. Wakefield asked.

"No, I set the table, remember?"

"What about Prince Albert's walk?" her father asked.

"Oh, Liz agreed to walk him for me tonight," she replied airily. She avoided meeting Elizabeth's eyes. The "agreement" to walk their bois-

46

terous young Labrador retriever had come only after a long bout of pleading and cajoling.

Her mother shrugged. "Well, OK, sweetheart. But don't stay out too late."

"I won't. 'Bye!"

Within moments Jessica was out the door and in the driver's seat of the Fiat. She couldn't wait to see Lila and show her the letters Elizabeth had placed on her bed that afternoon.

Lila lived in the most exclusive area of town—on the hill overlooking Sweet Valley, as did Bruce Patman's family and Regina Morrow's. As Jessica drove up the winding road, she passed stately mansions, separated from each other by discreet hedges and wide, manicured lawns. Here and there she glimpsed a swimming pool set amid landscaped grounds. Soon the gates of Fowler Crest came into view, and Jessica turned the convertible's nose up the long sweep of a driveway.

Lila met her at the door with a quizzical smile. "So what's the emergency meeting all about?"

Unconsciously Jessica's hand went to her shoulder bag, as if checking that the seven precious letters were still there. She smiled gleefully.

"I wanted you to help me go through my first batch of admirers," she said as she followed Lila up the grand staircase of the Spanish-style villa. She added sweetly, "I'm sure you'll start getting yours soon."

Lila led the way into her bedroom and shut the door behind Jessica. "Well, let's see them."

47

The two girls threw themselves down onto Lila's luxurious queen-sized bed and tore open the envelopes. Several minutes went by in silence; they exchanged letters without speaking until each of them had read every one.

Jessica ran the tip of her tongue over her lips. "So, what do you think?"

"Oh, I don't know," Lila drawled. She rolled off the bed and strolled to her cluttered vanity table. With slow, deliberate strokes, she pulled her brush through her silky, light brown hair. Finally she shrugged. "They're OK, I guess."

"OK?" Jessica shrieked, her indignation rising. She grabbed what she thought was the most promising letter, strode to her friend's side, and began reading aloud.

Dear Miss Excitement:

I'm no stranger to boasting, but I get the feeling you know how to put your money where your mouth is. You definitely sound like dynamite about to go off, and I want to be there for the explosion, even if it means getting a little singed. The girls I've met at college are nothing compared with someone like you.

I like slow dancing and romantic dinners. And I like dessert, too. . . .

Drop me a line. I think we should get together, *mi amore.*

Jessica regarded Lila's reflection in the mirror. "Doesn't that just give you goose bumps?" she demanded.

Lila shrugged again, infuriating Jessica even further. Lila acted so superior sometimes.

"Maybe it gives *you* goose bumps," Lila said, "but it gives me a rash! He sounds way too conceited to me."

"Conceited? Lila, for your information this guy is obviously incredibly *sexy* and *sophisticated*. He's not some shy little dork, you know."

Lila's answer was to pick up her hairbrush again.

"And you did notice that he speaks Italian, didn't you?"

"Jessica, anybody could learn two words of Italian. Give me a break."

Jessica turned away and flopped back onto the bed. She reread the letter yet again. The unmistakable promise in the word "dessert" sent a thrill of anticipation running up and down her spine.

As she pulled a pad of paper toward her, she said over her shoulder, "I'm writing back to him. And just you wait. If I date this guy, it's going to turn out to be the biggest romance of the century."

A week later Kirk Anderson sauntered out to the tennis courts after school, a huge grin on his face. He stood by the benches and nodded at Michael Harris, who left off making practice serves and jogged over to him. In another minute Neil Freemount walked up, and then they were joined by Chad Ticknor and Ron Reese.

"The ever-charming Jamie has another letter from the mystery girl," Kirk announced, drawing an envelope from his pocket with a dramatic flourish.

Michael grinned. "She's getting pretty devoted, huh? What's that, the third letter so far?"

"Go on, Kirk," said Ron. "Read it."

But Kirk held up one hand in a self-effacing gesture. "No, I think Neil should have the honor. After all, he's the one who's been doing all the work, right Neil?"

Neil felt a strange rush of pride and elation whenever Kirk singled him out like that. He knew Kirk was pretty obnoxious at times, but he also had a kind of charisma, a way of making a guy feel like part of a special, elite group. Although he had friends on the tennis team, he had never been part of a group. He was well liked but had always been regarded as somewhat of a loner. And Neil loved feeling as if he belonged.

That was why, when Kirk decided they should all get together and answer that crazy personal ad, he was glad to do most of the writing. Besides, whoever the girl was, she struck Neil— struck all of them—as being really funny and clever. And when he sat down to answer her letters, he unconsciously responded with his own brand of wit. It was like a long, drawn-out game, and the other guys loved it.

The only problem was, he was starting to wish he could write to this girl without his friends getting in on the act anymore. He couldn't figure out who in their school had placed the ad, but he really wanted to know. He was starting to feel as if it weren't a joke anymore, but couldn't bring himself to admit it to Kirk and the others.

"Go on, Neil. Let's see what old Quasimodo has to say today." Kirk held out the letter, a look of challenge in his brilliant blue eyes.

Neil took the envelope and returned Kirk's cynical smile, acting as nonchalant about it as he could. "Sure."

The boys watched as he slid his finger under the flap of the envelope and drew out the folded stationery. A wave of frustration washed over him as he noticed their predatory, eager smiles, but he forced himself to ignore it and began reading aloud.

Dear Jamie,

You're right. Sweet Valley does sometimes remind me of something from a movie—a Walt Disney movie! Do you ever go to the beach and just watch people? They're like a bunch of extras for some kind of beach-blanket movie. But as Shakespeare said, 'All the world's a stage,' right? Only if he was alive now he'd probably say 'All the world's a Hollywood set.' That Bill Shakespeare called it like he saw it.

But at the same time I love it here—I wouldn't want to live anywhere else. Do you feel that way, too? Except maybe I'd like living in a dark sixth-floor walk-up in some rundown section of New York City. Apparently every struggling writer is supposed to go through that kind of experience. Boy, doesn't that sound like fun? I guess as long as I could send out for pizza, I wouldn't mind.

You'll think this sounds stupid, but sometimes I wish I could be everywhere at once. I guess it does sound dumb. But I want to see everything, travel, meet all kinds of people, really live. But knowing me, I'll probably just get it out of books. Maybe one day I'll surprise myself, though. I'm doing a pretty good job of surprising myself just by writing to you, so who knows?

Write soon,

Q.

A chorus of laughter finished off Neil's reading of the letter, and Neil forced himself to smile. He knew they were laughing because parts of the letter were funny—but they were also laughing because to them it was one big joke that this girl was taking "Jamie" so seriously.

"I wish we could figure out who she is," Chad said, casually bouncing a ball on his racket. He shrugged. "Maybe we could try to meet her."

"Hey, now that's a great idea," Kirk said. He turned to Neil again. "Write another letter to her and set up some kind of meeting. Tell her that Jamie is dying to meet her."

"Yeah," Michael put in. "But let's make it somewhere where we can check her out first."

Neil bit the side of his thumb, a frown creasing his forehead. "Well . . ." It was a great idea, but he'd really rather meet her alone. Of course, there was no way he could keep the guys from going, too. "How about at the mall?"

"Good," Kirk decided, holding out his hand for Ron's notebook. He ripped out a sheet of paper and gave it to Neil. "Make it Friday. The day after tomorrow."

Neil dropped his racket and sat on one of the benches, composing the letter in his mind. Then he pulled a pen out of his pocket and began to write.

Dear Q.:

Every time I get another letter from you, I'm more and more convinced we should get together. I think it's time we met in person, don't you? If you want to meet me as much as I want to meet you, wait outside the bookstore in the mall at four o'clock on Friday. And wear something red so I'll know it's you.

If you don't come, I'll understand.

Jamie.

Neil almost wished she wouldn't come. He hated the idea of her being "checked out" first by the group. It meant if her looks didn't measure up to standard, they would give her the thumbs-down. And Neil instinctively knew she was a thumbs-up girl.

In fact, Neil was sure she was a girl he would really be able to talk to—unlike lots of girls he had dated. It seemed as if half of them were just interested in looking good or making out. A good, honest conversation was pretty hard to come by. He'd give anything for a chance to meet this girl in person.

"Well, this should do it, huh?" he said casually, holding it out.

Kirk took the letter and grinned. "Perfect. I can't wait till Friday."

"I just can't wait until Friday," Jessica announced as she pulled a scarf from Elizabeth's top drawer. She held the teal-blue silk up to her face and pouted her lips seductively, studying the effect in the mirror. "Can I borrow this for tomorrow night?"

"Sure." Elizabeth sighed and looked wistfully at her journal. Thursday afternoon was one of her usual times to catch up on her personal writing, but it didn't look as if she would have much of a chance with Jessica in one of her melodramatic moods.

Jessica squealed with delight and rushed over to hug her twin. "Oh, Lizzie, you're such an angel." She lounged on the bed next to Elizabeth and heaved a dramatic sigh. "You don't know what it's like to live with such suspense."

Elizabeth couldn't resist a wicked grin as she said, "With you around, Jess, I've been living in suspense for sixteen years."

Her twin sent her a withering look. "I'm talking about real *romantic* suspense, knowing that the man of your dreams is going to walk through the door tomorrow night. And then it will be history!"

"Actually, the man of my dreams should be walking through the door any minute now. Jeffrey and I are meeting Susan Stewart and Allen Walters at the Dairi Burger."

Jessica pushed herself up and stalked across the room, ignoring her sister. "I'm telling you, Liz. Paolo sounds like an absolute hunk."

"How can you tell he's a hunk just through his letters?"

"I can tell, Liz. Trust me. Anyway, he's very sophisticated."

Frowning, Elizabeth asked, "Do you know how old he is?" She leaned over the side of her bed to tickle Prince Albert's chest. He thumped his tail on the rug.

Jessica shrugged loftily. "He's in college. What

55

difference does age make when it's true romance?"

Most of Jessica's dates with college boys had turned out to be disasters, and Elizabeth felt she should remind her sister of that tiny detail. "You haven't had too much success with older men, you know. I think they're *too* sophisticated for you."

"You make them sound like they're a bunch of animals, Liz. Come on!" Jessica jumped up from the bed, went over to the mirror, and wound the blue scarf around her throat. "Have you forgotten our own brother happens to be in college? And I haven't heard Cara saying anything about him being a wild beast."

One of Jessica's best friends, Cara Walker, was going with Steven Wakefield. It was a romance Jessica had worked hard to arrange, and then had tried just as hard to break up, for her own obscure reasons. But Steven and Cara were a strong and steady couple, despite Jessica's efforts.

Elizabeth shook her head uncertainly. "I don't know, Jess. You keep trying to date older guys, and then when you do, it turns out to be a big mistake."

"But, Liz," Jessica insisted, "that's why I used a personal ad. All the other times it was just a superficial attraction; this time I really know something about him, and I'm *sure* we'll be a perfect match. That's the best part of doing it this way."

Elizabeth shrugged. She still wasn't convinced,

but there wasn't much use arguing with Jessica once her mind was made up. "Well, if you're sure, Jess." She glanced down at her open journal again. "Do Mom and Dad know you're going out with someone in college?"

A wary look crossed Jessica's face. "They're going out to dinner tomorrow night. I don't think they'll be around to find out. And you wouldn't tell them, would you?" she added with a winsome smile.

How did she always wind up in this situation? Elizabeth wondered to herself. Covering up for her adventure-seeking twin had been a way of life for as long as she could remember. But all things considered, she wouldn't have it any other way. She would stick by Jessica, no matter what.

"Don't worry, Jess. I won't tell them."

"Thanks, Liz," Jessica said happily. She gave her sister a brilliant smile, then disappeared into the bathroom that connected their rooms.

Elizabeth sighed and picked up her pen again. She wrote:

I thought this personal idea was a good one at first, but now I'm not so sure. Penny absolutely has stars in her eyes now that she's finally going to meet Jamie (whoever he is!), and I sure hope for her sake he turns out to be everything she expects. And now Jessica is going on a date with someone she doesn't know the least thing about.

But maybe I'm just being a pessimist. Who knows, maybe it will all turn out perfectly after all.

She closed her journal and stared moodily into Prince Albert's warm brown eyes as she added a postscript, "I'd better keep my fingers crossed."

Five

At three o'clock that Friday afternoon the five boys piled out of Kirk's white Trans Am. The parking lot at the Valley Mall was crowded, and they dodged around the cars, laughing and shouting jokes at one another as they made their way to the big main entrance.

"It's a good thing we came early," Ron said, yanking open the glass doors. "If she turns out to be a loser, we can split."

Michael grinned broadly. "Yeah. What if she really is a hunchback, after all?"

"I don't know, Harris. She sounds like your type." Chad ducked as Michael took a swing at him.

Neil frowned. He had his own opinion, but he was keeping it to himself. Describing herself that way told Neil a few things. First and foremost, it was obvious that she wasn't vain. No one with a huge ego would willingly cut it down that way. And she probably wasn't unattractive, either. In his experience, unattractive people were too sensitive to make jokes about their looks.

So where did that leave this one? He suspected that she was average-looking. Not a knockout, but attractive enough. After dating a handful of very pretty girls, Neil knew there was a lot more to a relationship than that.

He dug his hands deeper into his jeans pockets and said nothing as the others clowned around him.

Supremely aloof, Kirk strode through the crowded atrium with an unmistakable swagger, looking right and left with a casual, condescending glance. He had an air of command about him that showed him as their natural leader. The other boys walked slightly behind him.

When they reached the bookstore, they stopped, and Kirk crossed his arms, surveying the area. He jerked his head upward. "Let's go hang out up there," he said, indicating the mezzanine level. The spot would afford a perfect view of the bookstore entrance, and they could easily watch from up there without appearing to be waiting for anyone.

Neil cleared his throat. "Hey, why don't you all just wait at the video arcade, and I'll let you know how it goes."

"No way, Freemount," Kirk said. "Just because you're the lucky guy who's going to meet her doesn't mean we can't get in on the action, too."

With a shrug, Neil gave in. He hoped he looked as casual as he was trying to be. But his stomach was in knots. Sure, he had been elected to be the one who would go meet the girl, since he had done the most writing. But the others insisted on watching. And it really disturbed him that they would be lurking up above there, laughing at him while he met the girl he had such high hopes for.

"Besides," Kirk went on, smiling arrogantly, "if she turns out to be good-looking, I may go meet her myself. Maybe I'll take her to that Swing Fling dance. If you don't mind," he added with elaborate politeness.

"Jeez, man, I don't care," Neil replied quickly.

Kirk shot him a quick, piercing glance. Then he laughed and nodded toward the stairs. "Come on. Let's go up and wait." Hands in his pockets, Kirk sauntered over to the wide staircase and strolled up.

For a moment Neil felt a strong urge to stop him. But he couldn't help being impressed by Kirk's air of self-confidence: He acted as though he owned the mall and everyone in it. A grudging admiration filled him, and he followed the others up the stairs. He didn't want to do anything that would jeopardize his position with the group.

                    *   *   *

"Are you sure I look all right?" Penny asked
as they approached the mall entrance. It was
the fifth time she had repeated the question.

"Penny! Yes, you look great." Elizabeth assured her. Enid shot Penny a quick, sympa-
thetic smile and reached forward to pull open
the heavy glass door.

Briefly, as the door swung toward her, Penny
caught a glimpse of her reflection in the glass.
She was wearing a new denim skirt, slightly
shorter than the skirts she usually wore. She
had to admit it showed her legs to advantage.
And the colorful, madras camp shirt she had on
brought out the pink in her lightly blushed
cheeks. In her hair was a bright red headband
that pulled back her short, straight hair and
gave it a gentle, forward-sweeping curve. She
couldn't remember the last time she had made
such an effort with her appearance. *I just hope it
pays off*, she said to herself.

Then they were inside the busy mall. Penny
glanced at the big atrium clock: 3:55. Five more
minutes and she would actually meet *him*.

"OK, Penny. We're going to do some shop-
ping," Elizabeth was saying. She checked her
watch. "We'll hang around until five-thirty, then
meet you in front of Lisette's. Will that give you
enough time?"

"Well, I'd like to say no," Penny answered

with a faint glimmer of her usual, wry sense of humor. "But I'm trying to be realistic."

Enid squeezed her arm. "Good luck. I bet he turns out to be fantastic."

As they turned to go, Penny felt her heart begin to pound. It was really happening!

She took a deep breath, then walked down the long right-hand aisle of the atrium to the bookstore. The window was filled with books on display—best-sellers, new home-improvement books, books by local authors. There were several she meant to read, and any other time she would have gone in to browse. But not today.

She rocked back on her heels and glanced quickly around. Standing there made her feel very self-conscious, and she stared into the window with intense concentration. One book cover showed a man and a woman, both in nineteenth-century costume, locked in a passionate embrace, and Penny felt her cheeks grow hot as she looked at it.

Any minute now Jamie would arrive, and Penny knew he would be perfect. His letters showed he had imagination and character, and he responded to everything that was really important to her. Penny knew she was already halfway to falling in love with him. She had painted a picture of him in her mind: He would be attractive in an interesting way, and athletic, strong . . .

Out of the corner of her eye, she became

aware of someone approaching, and she turned with a tremendous smile. A tall, blond boy was walking toward her, a look of expectation in his eyes.

Penny opened her mouth to speak but shut it with a snap as he walked right by her into the bookstore. A hot flush of embarrassment washed over her as she realized she had almost made a complete fool of herself.

A quick glance at her watch showed her it was four-ten, and she frowned anxiously. Where was he? A niggling whisper of panic battled with her common sense, and she searched her mind frantically for a reason he might be late. Car trouble, she told herself. Maybe his watch was slow. Besides, ten minutes wasn't so late. *He'll be here*, she told herself.

She folded her arms and nervously tapped her fingers on her elbows. She tried not to look at her watch. She looked everywhere but at her watch.

"Penny!"

She spun around, her heart pounding, to see Sally Larson and her boyfriend Mark Riley. Penny felt her face flush crimson.

"Waiting for someone?" Sally asked, a friendly smile on her face.

"Uh . . . yeah." Penny swallowed painfully.

An awkward silence descended suddenly, and Penny noticed a puzzled frown on Mark's face. "I—I'm meeting someone here," she stammered.

Sally nodded. "Well, see you later."

The two disappeared into the crowd, and Penny drew a deep breath. She couldn't believe how on edge and nervous she was.

Every once in a while someone would slow down to enter the bookstore, and each time Penny's heartbeat accelerated. But no one stopped to speak to her.

Soon she just had to look at her watch again; she couldn't help it. And she felt a growing surge of anxiety when she saw it was four-thirty. He wouldn't be that late, would he? Especially when it was his idea to meet in the first place?

Then a sickening thought occurred to her. Maybe he *had* been right on time. What if he had already arrived and seeing who she was, decided to leave? Standing there with the vivid red headband in her hair, Penny realized she was easily recognizable. But since she didn't know who Jamie was, he could have walked right by her, and she never would have known the difference.

If Jamie was someone from Sweet Valley High, he could have seen it was she, Penny Ayala, and gotten turned off. After all, she reasoned, boys didn't like to go out with girls like her. Her own love life to date was proof enough of that.

So that's that, she told herself firmly. *I'll just leave.* But then it occurred to her that if she left now, she would never know who Jamie was—assuming he did show up, after all.

At twenty minutes to five, Penny decided he just wasn't going to turn up. Resolutely she turned to walk away. Before she had taken ten steps, however, a thought flashed into her mind: *What if he suddenly shows up after I've gone?* She turned slowly to walk back to the bookstore. But ten minutes later she gave up hope. No one could be forty-five minutes late. Jamie didn't want to meet her after all.

Penny had never felt worse in her life. She turned and walked blindly through the crowded mall to the entrance. Someone bumped into her, but Penny didn't even look up. Her one thought was escape. When the bus came, she climbed aboard as if she were in a trance and sat huddled in a seat by the window. As the bus gave a wheezing gasp and pulled out of the parking lot, Penny felt hot tears sliding down her cheeks.

"Jessica! How long are you going to take in there?" Elizabeth caught her breath as she stepped into the bathroom. There was so much steam in the air, she could hardly see the shower.

"Just one more minute!" Jessica sang out.

I bet, Elizabeth said silently, and shot a good-natured grimace at the shower curtain. She wiped off a patch on the mirror and studied her eyes.

The new, smoky-blue shade of eyeliner she had bought at the mall that afternoon was subtle, but effective. She wasn't as vain as her twin, but Elizabeth liked to look good. She smiled as she thought of what Jeffrey's reaction might be when he picked her up later.

Penny and Jamie must have really hit it off, she mused, thinking happily back on the events of the afternoon. Elizabeth and Enid had waited until a quarter to six, and when Penny still hadn't shown up, they decided that she and Jamie were so absorbed in each other that they had lost track of time.

Elizabeth glanced at her watch. She was sure Jessica would still be drenching herself in hot water for another ten minutes, so she had plenty of time for a quick call.

Elizabeth went into her room, reached for the phone, and quickly dialed the Ayalas' number.

Penny's mother answered.

"Hi, this is Elizabeth Wakefield. Is Penny there?"

There was a short silence before Mrs. Ayala responded. "Well . . . she said she wasn't feeling well, Elizabeth. But I'm sure she'd want to talk to you. I'll go get her."

I wonder if something's wrong, Elizabeth thought, suddenly feeling uneasy.

Elizabeth wrapped the coiled phone cord around her index finger as she waited. There was an unusually long pause before Penny finally picked up the phone.

"Hi, Liz." her voice was subdued.

"Penny, how did it go? Did you and Jamie get along pretty well?"

With a shaky laugh, Penny said, "Pretty well? He didn't even show up, Liz."

Elizabeth felt as if she'd been punched in the stomach. *Poor Penny!* "Oh, Penny, I'm so sorry!" Elizabeth exclaimed.

"Yeah, me too."

"Well, what happened?"

A dejected sigh came across the line. "I don't know. I waited for a whole hour, and he never came."

Elizabeth's mind raced. "He must have run into some kind of emergency, Penny, and didn't know how to get a message to you."

"Maybe. I don't know."

Obviously, Penny was not convinced that was the explanation.

"Maybe—" Elizabeth began.

"Liz, I think he just took one look at me and did an about-face. I guess I should have expected it."

"Don't say that! Penny, there has to be a logical explanation for why he didn't come. I know there is."

"Thanks, Liz. I know you're just trying to help, but I know what happened. He said, 'Oh, God, it's Penny Ayala,' and took off. Sometimes I wish I was just some dumb blond cheerleader, or—" She broke off with a gasp. "I'm sorry, Liz, I didn't mean—"

Elizabeth laughed ruefully. "I know you didn't mean Jessica, Penny. Don't worry about it. But don't ever say you wish you were dumb. You're bright and funny and interesting, and Jamie doesn't know what he's missing."

There was a short pause, and Penny finally said, "Well, maybe he does. And he's probably congratulating himself right now on getting out of a bad situation. Boy, imagine getting stuck with me!"

With her friend in this kind of mood, Elizabeth knew there really wasn't anything she could say. All she could do was let Penny know she was there for her.

"Well, I'll see you Monday, OK?"

"Sure, Liz. 'Bye."

Elizabeth hung up the phone slowly and stood up, deep in thought. If only there was something she could do! But there wasn't. She heard the water finally stop running in the bathroom and decided it was time for a hot shower.

Six

Jessica wrapped a fluffy towel around her and stepped over to the fogged-up mirror.

"So, is there any hot water left for me?" Elizabeth said as she walked into the bathroom.

"Oh, Liz, you're such a riot." Jessica laughed airily and stared hard at her reflection. Her full attention was focused on one thing and one thing only: how to look absolutely sensational for the mysterious Paolo.

She switched on the blow dryer as Elizabeth turned on the shower. Jessica's silky gold locks blew around her face, giving her a careless wind-swept look that so many fashion models seemed to favor. It was a look that could appear either messy or sophisticated, and Jessica decided that if anybody could pull it off successfully, she could.

Armed with a can of styling mousse and

a brush, she worked on her hair with the concentration of a brain surgeon. At last she achieved what she thought was the perfect balance: her hair was swept back from her face except for a few carefully chosen tendrils, which curled forward, suggesting rumpled abandon. The effect was sultry and vaguely European.

On the edge of the sink was Elizabeth's brand new blue eyeliner stick. She picked it up, admiring the color. It was exactly right for her.

She cast a quick look over her shoulder at the shower curtain and figured her twin wouldn't mind if she used it. She peered into the mirror again, then outlined her eyes carefully, smudging and blending the smoky color until she had it just right. Her eyes looked enormous. The pencil was blunted terribly, but she knew Elizabeth could always sharpen it again, so Jessica put it out of her mind.

At last satisfied with her hair and her makeup, Jessica waltzed back into her bedroom to get dressed.

Hands on her hips, she studied her wardrobe. She wanted to look grown-up but innocent, sophisticated but casual. And above all, sexy. From his letters, Jessica had the impression that Paolo was one of those passionate European men who liked their women ultrafeminine. And ultrafeminine was what Jessica intended to be.

She chose a skimpy white tank top in a nubbly

silk knit, and a straight, figure-hugging blue linen skirt. She knotted Elizabeth's teal blue scarf around her throat, then stepped into a pair of thin-strapped white sandals.

"Look out, Paolo." She smiled with satisfaction as she surveyed the effect in her full-length mirror.

She heard her twin moving around in the bathroom. "How do I look?" she sang out.

Elizabeth poked her head around the door, and her eyes widened. "Wow! Jess, you look fantastic!"

"Do I really?" Jessica knew she did, but she couldn't resist asking. "Are you sure?"

"Absolutely. When's Paolo picking you up?"

Jessica turned to look at her reflection from the side. "What time is it now?"

"Seven."

Dabbing her best perfume on her wrists, Jessica said, "Oh, he should be here now, then. And, Liz, if you don't mind," she added sweetly, "I'd prefer to make a solo entrance, if you know what I mean."

"Sure, Jess. I'll meet him *after* he's fallen in love with you. Good luck."

Luck has nothing to do with it, Jessica thought as she walked down the stairs.

When the door bell rang, she strolled into the front hall, arranging her features into what she hoped was an expression of world-weary sophistication.

"Paolo," she murmured as she pulled open the door. And then she froze.

Standing in the doorway was an undeniably overweight boy. Assuming that he couldn't possibly be her date, she looked past him to the street.

"Jessica? Hi, I'm Paolo. I'm so glad to meet you."

She shook herself, trying to overcome her shock. He was actually holding out one perfect long-stemmed rose. "Uh . . ."

With a quizzical smile, he suggested, "Maybe you should put it in water."

"Water! Right! I'll be right back!" Flustered and panicked, Jessica slammed the door and raced into the kitchen. What was she going to do?"

Never in her life had Jessica ever dated anyone who wasn't handsome and slim. And now she was going out with—with—someone *fat*.

She couldn't go through with it. What if someone saw her with him? Her reputation would be ruined! What if Lila found out? She would never let Jessica forget it in ten million years.

Besides, it was perfectly clear that she wasn't going to win the contest with Paolo, so going out with him was a total waste of a Friday night. She just had to think of some way to get out of her date. She'd find some excuse, some explanation.

The sound of footsteps upstairs galvanized

her into action. An explanation would take time, and that was exactly what she didn't have. If Elizabeth saw him . . .

She threw the rose into the sink and tore back through the house to the front door. " 'Bye!" she called over her shoulder as she yanked the door open. Grabbing Paolo's arm, she dragged him to the Camaro parked at the curb. "Come on! Let's go."

"I guess you really do like to move fast." He chuckled as he settled himself in behind the steering wheel. He glanced at her, an amused look on his face.

Jessica could hardly look at him, she was so frantic about thinking up a good excuse. But she forced herself to smile. "I thought you were Italian."

He laughed as he started up the car and pulled away from the house. "Well, my parents are, but I've lived in California all my life."

Great, thought Jessica. *So much for a sophisticated European.*

"And I bet you're wondering about—" He paused, and glanced at her again. "Well, I'm not exactly a devastatingly handsome guy," he admitted.

She laughed nervously and couldn't think of a single thing to say. She could hardly deny a statement of such obvious truth.

"But I figure it doesn't bother me that I'm a

little heavy—I just love to eat. And speaking of eating, I made reservations for us at Tiborino's."

Jessica gulped. Tiborino's. That was the most fashionable Italian restaurant in the valley, and one of her parents' favorite spots. All she could do was pray there wasn't anyone there she knew, or who might recognize her.

She clenched her hands together and stared out the window, letting Paolo talk without bothering to listen. She had to come up with some reason to cut this date off at the earliest possible moment. Then maybe she'd be able to go to the Beach Disco and try to salvage the night.

"Astronomy," Paolo was saying. "It's really fascinating. I've been studying black holes this semester. You know, they're so dense and have such a strong gravitational pull that they suck everything around them inside, even light."

"Neat," Jessica said tightly.

"And here we are." Paolo maneuvered the car into a parking space outside the restaurant and gave her a friendly smile. "Ready?"

"Sure."

Jessica cringed inwardly as he took her arm walking up the steps, and she made a fuss about searching in her purse as he spoke with the maitre d'. That way she could keep her head down and her face hidden, and if all went well, she could get to their table without anyone seeing her.

"Do you think we could sit in one of the booths?" she whispered hoarsely.

He raised his eyebrows, surprised. The back end of the room was dark and romantic, and Jessica realized with a sinking heart that he must think she really liked him! But she could take care of that later.

Paolo turned back to the maitre d', who nodded to the spoken request, then led them through the crowded dining room to a booth in back. Jessica breathed a sigh of relief and then buried her face in her menu.

"How about if I order for both of us?" Paolo suggested, noticing her anxiety and misinterpreting it. A waiter appeared as if by magic, and Paolo spoke to him in rapid Italian.

"So, tell me a little about yourself," Paolo began after the waiter had left. He unfolded his napkin and looked at her with an interested smile. "I already know you're the prettiest girl in the restaurant."

"Well . . ." She faltered, toying with the salt shaker. What was she going to do? She suddenly felt like throwing up. That would be a pretty spectacular solution. Then she had a brilliant idea. "I . . . actually, I've been sort of an invalid all my life," she lied, the words coming easily now that she knew what course to take.

"You're kidding? But you look so healthy."

"Oh? Well, looks can be deceiving, I guess.

76

Anyway, I get these terrible headaches—I had a CAT scan yesterday, in fact. I'll know in a few days whether it's—it's—" She broke off dramatically and tried to look brave.

Paolo froze with a breadstick halfway to his mouth. "Whether it's—?"

Jessica affected a careless shrug. "But I like to ignore the pain when I can. Life is just too short."

Paolo was obviously moved. "Jessica, I had no idea. What you must go through! But you're OK right now, aren't you?"

Jessica allowed the briefest hesitation to hang in the air. "Oh. Yes. . . Yes—I'm OK." Her voice dropped, and she lowered her eyes to her lap.

"You're so brave. I can't tell you how much I admire you, Jessica. You're really remarkable."

Jessica ducked her head a little lower to hide a smile. Once she got going, she *was* pretty remarkable. A few more minutes of this and she'd be out of that restaurant: Paolo would never know what hit him.

"No, I'm not really," she whispered. She looked up and gave him a dazzling smile. Then the slightest flicker of pain crossed her face.

He was instantly alert. "Are you sure you're feeling OK?"

"Paolo, I . . ." A picture of confusion, Jessica shook her head. "I just wanted to have fun like any normal girl. For once! Instead of staying

home and taking medicines and—'' She closed
her eyes and gasped, raising a trembling hand
to her forehead. She wondered briefly if conjur-
ing up a few tears would be going a little too
far.

Throwing his napkin down, Paolo jumped to
his feet and took her arm. ''Come on, Jessica.
Don't do this to yourself. Let me take you home.''

''I—no.'' She stood up, looking as reluctant
as possible. ''Well, I guess maybe you should.
I'm so sorry, though, Paolo. All those things I
said. I just wanted—''

''Don't worry about it, really. I'm a stupid
jerk for not noticing earlier that you didn't feel
well. When you answered the door you looked—
well, kind of dazed.''

''Dazed'' is not the word! thought Jessica.

Within minutes they were driving quickly back
through downtown Sweet Valley and then
through that residential neighborhood where
the Wakefields lived. Jessica kept one hand
pressed to her forehead throughout the ride.

Finally, after many more protests that she
would be all right after a few days' rest, Jessica
got Paolo to agree to leave her alone in the
house without calling a doctor. When he asked
her if he could see her again, she murmured,
''I'll let you know if—that is, if I don't have to
go to the—''

''You're wonderful, Jessica,'' Paolo replied.
''It's been an honor just meeting you. I'm only

sorry it didn't work out this time. But give me a call when you're feeling better."

With a last, lingering look, Paolo got back into his car and drove away. Jessica waved one hand delicately before letting herself in the door.

"Whew!" Jessica leaned against the door and started to giggle. "That must have been the fastest ditch on record." She laughed out loud.

She frowned as a little voice inside told her she'd just played a mean trick on a polite, friendly, and interesting boy. But she ignored the voice. After all, she couldn't help it if she simply couldn't stand to be around fat people.

A complaining grumble from her stomach reminded Jessica that she hadn't eaten yet, and she wandered through the silent, empty house to the kitchen. Prince Albert lifted his head from his basket by the patio door and wagged his tail. Then he got up and ambled over to her.

"Hi, good boy," Jessica crooned, fondling his silky ears. "You won't tell anybody what time I got home, now will you?"

On the table was a bud vase with the single rose in it. Next to it a note was propped.

Dear Jess:
  I guess you were in a hurry to go out with Paolo, so I took care of this rose for you. By the way, if you're still interested, I

found some more responses to your ad that I forgot to give you. Sorry.

Love,
Liz.

"No more blind dates!" Jessica groaned, helping herself to a glass of orange juice. "Thank you very much."

She sat down at the table and looked skeptically at the pile of envelopes as Prince Albert put his head on her knee and looked up at her adoringly. Her first attempt had been a certifiable disaster, and she didn't feel like taking that kind of risk again. But on the other hand, she did have that contest with Lila. She couldn't back out of it, and she sure wouldn't win with a tub of lard like Paolo!

"I guess I'd better check these out," she muttered.

Wrinkling her nose with disgust, Jessica tore open the letter at the top of the pile. A photograph fell out, and she picked it up.

The picture was a Polaroid close-up, like a passport picture. And the face was the kind she'd love to get close to! The boy was deeply tanned, with warm brown eyes and thick, wavy blond hair. In a word he was gorgeous. At once Jessica began to read the letter:

Hi:
I read your personal ad the other day,

80

and I have to confess, I was hooked! You sound like a fun, exciting girl with a sense of adventure, and that's what I like. I know a lot of people exaggerate when they describe themselves in an ad, but for some reason, I got the feeling you haven't! And I'd love to find out if I'm right.

I've enclosed a picture of myself because I know some girls are cautious about dating guys they've never seen. I'm a college freshman, and I love to surf and play tennis. Would you like to take a chance with me?

My name is John Karger, and you can get in touch with me through the sociology department at the university. Drop me a line—maybe we can get together.

Jessica lowered the letter thoughtfully and picked up the photograph again. John Karger, eh? From his letter he seemed like an honest, straightforward guy, a guy she could really get used to. And from his photograph, she knew there wouldn't be any nasty surprises! If the competition with Lila was going to be won on looks, this candidate was definitely way out in front.

"OK, John Karger, let's see what you're made of," she said reaching for the note pad by the phone.

As she wrote up a rough draft of her response to John, she smiled. She would go out with John but would hold off telling Lila about him until she'd had her first date. After all, she had made such a big fuss over Paolo that she was going to have a hard time explaining why he hadn't worked out.

So, if by some strange chance John turned out to be a loser, Lila would never know. But if he looked as if he'd be Jessica's winning date, well, there was plenty of time to tell Lila about him *afterward*.

And for the time being, the night was still young. . . .

Jessica chuckled and went upstairs to change her clothes.

Seven

"Hey, Freemount! Over here!"

Kirk Anderson's voice rang out across the cafeteria. Neil couldn't help feeling pleased and a little smug that he'd been singled out so publicly. It almost made up for Friday afternoon. Almost.

He pulled out a chair at the table and started to eat his hamburger, listening idly to the other boys around him. But he stiffened when he heard the conversation turn.

"Man, I almost died when it turned out to be Penny Ayala." Chad groaned, then took a swallow of milk from a carton. "Can you believe it?"

Kirk grinned maliciously. "No kidding. I haven't been here long, but long enough to know which girls to stay away from. She's definitely one of them."

"Yeah. Miss Ace Student of Sweet Valley

High!" Ron put in. "Who'd want to date a girl who's always got her nose in her books?"

Michael chuckled. "Yeah. She'd probably be after you all the time to study. And I do enough of that as it is."

Kirk leaned across the table and punched Neil's shoulder. "We saved your tail the other day, Freemount. If we hadn't decided to watch from up on the second level, you'd have gotten nailed for sure!"

Neil smiled weakly, but he felt absolutely sick inside. Friday afternoon came back to him with vivid clarity. . . .

They were leaning over the railing, taking bets on what type of girl would show up and watching the bookstore entrance twenty feet below like hawks. When a cute blonde in a red shirt walked to the door, they all burst into appreciative laughter.

"I'll handle this!" Kirk announced, a gleam in his eye. "You kids stay here and watch how a pro handles the ladies."

But the girl had gone into the store and then reappeared a few minutes later, a package under one arm. She walked away.

And then Penny Ayala had arrived. She stood just below them, obviously waiting for someone outside the bookstore. At first Neil had looked past her, and then the bright red ribbon in her hair caught his attention. *Penny* had written those letters!

He couldn't believe it. She was in his American literature class, an elective for juniors and seniors, and he had always admired her comments and suggestions about the books they were reading. But she seemed so unapproachable. Penny had an air of superiority that he found intimidating. It wasn't that she was snobby or aloof, so much as so obviously above everyone else. She was in control, and she was keenly intelligent. He never would have dreamed that she was the funny, easy-going Quasimodo of their letters. Somewhat guiltily he realized that he had never thought of Penny as someone to date. But this put matters in a whole new light.

He was about to push away from the rail and go down to meet her when the astonished laughter of his friends stopped him in his tracks.

"Penny Ayala? You've got to be kidding!" Chad hooted, hiding a snicker behind his hand.

"Can you imagine going out with her? You'd probably end up writing a term paper on dates!"

"Or reading *War and Peace!*"

The other boys howled with laughter, and Neil felt himself wanting to yell, "But don't you see she isn't really like that? Her letters prove it!"

But he couldn't. Kirk was doing a wickedly funny impersonation of a prim schoolteacher that was obviously meant to be Penny. "Now class," he said, "the bonus question for today is: Who wants to escort me to the dance?"

Ron, Chad, and Michael burst out laughing. They slapped their knees and punched each others' arms. Kirk sent Neil a sharp, inquisitive look. "That was a close one, right?"

Neil had swallowed hard and nodded. "Sure was."

With a last lingering glance over the railing, he turned and followed his teammates down the stairs. The last Neil saw of Penny, she had been checking her watch with an anxious frown.

I'm sorry, he told her silently.

"Hey, I'm only sorry you weren't there, man," Kirk was saying to Tom McKay now. "And she was really dressed up." His voice was tinged with malicious scorn.

Tom frowned. "I don't get it—which one of you guys answered the ad?"

"It was all of us! That's why it was so funny! Of course, it was my idea to begin with," Kirk boasted, clearly proud of himself. "But Neil did most of the writing. He's really the one that got her turned on."

Neil's hamburger suddenly tasted awful. He pushed his tray away abruptly and stood up.

"I—I just remembered something I've got to do," he stammered, unable to look at or listen to Kirk another moment. "Catch you later."

He turned and stumbled away, his emotions in turmoil. He couldn't remember ever feeling so confused or upset about anything. At that moment he felt like the most detestable person in the world.

At the next table Elizabeth, who was having lunch with Enid, swallowed her root beer with difficulty. It took all her self-control not to turn around and throw the whole can right into Kirk's arrogant, conceited face. Enid was silent, her expression stormy.

Finally Elizabeth let out a long, shaky breath. "How could they?" she said. "How *could* they?"

I've never heard anything more despicable in my life."

Elizabeth gave a hasty glance over her shoulder to the next table. Kirk was still chuckling over what he thought was a great joke. He was actually congratulating himself. She couldn't think of anyone she had ever disliked so much.

"I knew he was a jerk the minute I laid eyes on him," Enid muttered fiercely. "But I never imagined how *much* of a jerk he truly is."

"What I can't understand is why Ron and Neil were in on it, though. Michael and Chad I can believe, but not those two."

Enid shrugged. "Well, you have to admit, that arrogant worm has a very strong personality. I can see them getting sucked into some kind of dumb practical joke if he was the ringleader."

Elizabeth's eyes widened, and she shook her

head with admiration. "You should study psychology when you go to college, Enid. You're probably right. But it doesn't make it any less cruel that they did it."

"True. But I do think there's really only one person responsible, and that's Kirk."

Frowning, Elizabeth took another long sip at her root beer. "I just wish there was some way to get even with him—for Penny's sake." She looked up and saw her twin coming toward her.

But before Jessica could reach her, she had to pass the table of tennis players, and Kirk Anderson caught her arm.

"Hey, Jess, how about doing yourself a favor and going out with me this weekend?"

Jessica snatched her arm away as though it had been burned. "Don't you touch me, you worm!" she hissed, her voice filled with loathing. "I wouldn't go out with you if my life depended on it."

Kirk threw his head back and roared with laughter as Jessica stalked away. She dumped her books next to Elizabeth and flung herself into a chair.

"He's got to be the biggest jerk in California," she seethed. "Maybe in the whole universe! Nobody talks to me that way!"

Elizabeth nodded grimly. She was surprised that Jessica was sitting with her and Enid, since Jessica never made any secret of her dislike for

Elizabeth's best friend. But she had a feeling Jessica was avoiding Lila. Apparently her date with Paolo was something she didn't look forward to telling Lila about.

At the next table Kirk's self-assured voice rose again over the noise. "The girl I take to this Swing Fling dance is going to be saying prayers of thanks."

Someone snorted. "Who's the lucky girl, Anderson?"

"I haven't decided yet. I like to take my time checking out the selection. But whoever I pick, you better believe she's going to be *hot*."

With an indignant snort, Jessica grabbed the copy of *Ingenue* she had thrown down with her notebook, and flipped angrily through the magazine. The pages snapped and almost ripped beneath her fingers, and her mouth was set in a stern line.

"I'd like to fix him," she muttered. "I can't believe what a first-class jerk he is." She threw the magazine on the table. "Ugh! He makes me want to puke."

The magazine fell open to a spread featuring a stunning, raven-haired young model with emerald green eyes and flawless skin. The paragraph underneath described the girl as one of New York's hottest new teen models, Erica Hall. Sixteen years old and breathtakingly beautiful, Erica lived in Manhattan and led a fabulous, jet-set life, posing for magazine spreads all over the world and going to glamorous parties with rock stars and princes.

Elizabeth stared at the photograph blankly, barely aware that she was even reading the caption. A hint of an idea began to form in the back of her mind as she picked up the magazine.

Enid saw the speculative look on her friend's face and raised one eyebrow. "Liz is thinking. I can see the wheels turning around in there."

Jessica grinned back at her. Their mutual antagonism dissolved as their overpowering dislike of Kirk Anderson and his arrogance forged a truce between the two girls. She leaned forward eagerly. "What is it, Liz?"

Elizabeth glanced back at Kirk for a second. "I think I know how to get him," she said, her voice low. She carefully ripped out the pages with Erica Hall's pictures. "Is this girl in any other magazines?" she asked softly.

Jessica's brow furrowed as she looked at the model. "Uh—yeah, I think so. Yes, she's on the cover of last month's *Ingenue*, and she's in *Mademoiselle* this month, too. Why?"

"Liz, what are you plotting?"

"Hey, girls," came a male voice behind them.

The three jumped guiltily, then relaxed when they saw Jeffrey. He sat down with them and grinned at Elizabeth. "You look like you're plotting a murder," he teased.

"You've got that right," Jessica declared. "Liz is going to get Kirk the Jerk."

Jeffrey's eyebrows went up a fraction. "What's going on?"

"Kirk Anderson is a low, mean, horrible jerk, and we're just going to teach him a little lesson," Elizabeth said softly, her voice intense with anger.

Jeffrey looked over his shoulder at Kirk. "You don't want me to beat him up or something, do you?"

"Yes!" shouted Jessica.

"No." Elizabeth couldn't help laughing. "Don't worry, Jeffrey. I'm not going to require your brute strength, so don't look so nervous. I've got a better way."

"So tell us, Liz!" Enid said excitedly. "I'm dying to know your idea!"

Elizabeth looked at Enid, then at Jessica. "If he wants hot, he'll get hot. This is an idea worthy of even you, Jess. We're going to give him a taste of his own medicine. And if all goes well, it'll be a dose he has a pretty tough time swallowing."

Eight

Neil slid into his seat in Mr. Collins's American literature class on Tuesday morning feeling as if he had to do something—anything. Across the room Penny sat in her usual place. Was it his imagination, or did she seem particularly subdued and serious, just as she had the day before? If she was, he had a pretty good idea who was responsible for making her so unhappy: he was.

He thumbed distractedly through his copy of *Huckleberry Finn*, trying to think of something he could say to her to clear up the stupid mess. But his mind was a blank.

"Hi, folks," Mr. Collins called out cheerfully, striding into the classroom. He tossed his books on his desk and walked to the blackboard to pick up a piece of chalk.

" 'Classic: a book that people praise and don't

read,' " he repeated as he scrawled the quotation on the blackboard.

He wiped his hands together and faced the class. "Just about the truest thing Mark Twain ever said," he continued with a grin. "But Twain didn't know at the time that *Huckleberry Finn* would become *the* American classic. And people do read it—and read it again and again.

"Now that presumably you've all read the first nine chapters, let's see if we can figure out why this book is so great. Any thoughts?" The handsome, enthusiastic teacher folded his arms and surveyed his class, an expectant smile turning up the corners of his mouth.

Notebooks shuffled and chairs scraped, but no one said a word. Mr. Collins rubbed his chin thoughtfully. "Hmm. Penny, how about you? What do you think of it?"

Penny sat up in her seat and flushed. Obviously her thoughts had been far away. "I'm sorry, I didn't hear the question," she said, and blushed even harder.

That's my fault, Neil silently cursed himself. He had to get her off the spot.

"I think it's because Huck epitomized everything good about America at the time," Neil cut in, hardly knowing where the words came from.

"Good. Very good, Neil." Mr. Collins smiled, turning from the distraught Penny at last. "Keep going. What characteristics make you say that?"

Neil paused. He wasn't in the habit of talking

much in class, even though he always had something to contribute if he felt like it. He just didn't want to very often. But now he did. He wanted Penny to know that he was an intelligent, thoughtful person.

"Well," he continued finally, "he's clever and streetwise, but he's also innocent and hopeful. And loyal to Jim, even though in that time it was wrong for him to be helping a runaway slave."

Mr. Collins smiled. "You put it very well, Neil. Huck is the spirit of America, then?"

Neil shrugged. "Yeah, I guess that's what I mean."

A warm glow of pride swept over Neil that was different from the feeling he got at being part of Kirk Anderson's group. Penny had glanced his way with an admiring look in her eyes. There might even have been a hint of relief and gratitude there too. He knew then that her approval and acceptance meant a whole lot more to him than Kirk's ever had or ever would.

There must be some way to explain, he thought. Maybe he could talk to her after class and apologize.

His decision suddenly lightened the sick feeling that had been weighing him down since Friday afternoon. He knew what to do, and he would do it.

When the bell rang, he maneuvered his way

into the crowd leaving the classroom and stood behind Penny. But he couldn't think of anything to say. She was right there in front of him. In another few seconds she would be out the door and down the hall, and the moment would be gone.

"Do you like the book?" he said at last, feeling a wave of humiliation wash over him as he heard how lame his question sounded. "*Huckleberry Finn*, I mean."

Penny turned her head and gave him a questioning glance. "Yeah," she said with a faint smile. "Mark Twain was a brilliant writer."

Then, abruptly, she turned back to the door.

This wasn't the Penny Ayala he knew, Neil realized with a shock. Usually Penny was shy, but at least she was always eager to talk about books. Now she seemed distant, even cold.

He stood rooted to the spot, letting the rest of the class surge out the door around him. He was responsible for the change in Penny, and he knew it. He was even more at fault than the other guys, because he had gone along with the prank, knowing that it was cruel and wrong. If Penny was wary now of any kind of relationship with a boy—even a casual conversation after class—then it was his fault. And it was up to him to remedy the situation.

Or was it up to "Jamie"? Maybe the best way to solve the problem was to have the guy she liked explain what happened—or not explain, exactly, but try to patch things up. With a quick nod, Neil decided that would be the thing to do.

His next class was study hall, and as soon as he had taken a seat, he pulled a sheet of paper from his notebook and composed one more letter from "Jamie."

Dear Q.:

How can I apologize for standing you up on Friday? An emergency came up, and there was no way I could get a message to you. I can only say how really sorry I am. I hope you can forgive me. I really don't want to lose this chance, because I think I know what a special person you are. Reading your letters and writing to you has really meant a lot to me, and I hope you feel the same way.

If you aren't completely turned off on me, could we try another meeting? I'll be waiting outside the Dairi Burger on Thursday afternoon at four. Don't answer this letter. I'll know on Thursday whether you've forgiven me or not.

Neil signed the letter "Jamie." That should do it, he thought. They could just start all over, pretend Friday never happened. He prayed silently that she wouldn't write back, since the box number they had been using was assigned to Kirk. Above all, Neil didn't want Kirk to know he was arranging to meet Penny.

All he could do now was wait until Thursday to see if the damage could be undone. As he carefully folded the letter, he fervently hoped that it could.

Penny pushed her way through the crowded hall until she got to the girls' room. She slipped inside with relief.

You're acting like an idiot, she told her reflection sternly. *You're acting as if this is the end of the world.*

Sighing heavily, Penny leaned against a sink and stared at the tile floor. The stilted conversation—if it could be called that—with Neil Freemount came back to her, and she shook her head with disgust. If she couldn't have a normal conversation with a boy, how was she ever going to go out with one?

But then again, if she could talk easily to a guy like Neil, she wouldn't be in this position in the first place. It was precisely because she had trouble acting natural and confident with boys that she had written that ad. And things had looked so promising when she started getting Jamie's letters.

Well, it was over, and she just wouldn't let it bother her anymore. She would concentrate on her schoolwork and just forget about pursuing a social life.

Who needs it anyway? she thought, knowing that she didn't mean it.

By lunchtime Elizabeth's plan was ready to be put into action. She and Enid scanned the cafeteria and spotted Kirk Anderson sitting at one of the tables by the windows. The table next to him was empty, and the two girls headed for it.

"Let's wait till things settle down a little," Elizabeth warned. She darted a look over Enid's shoulder to the tableful of noisy junior boys. Kirk was sitting directly behind Enid.

Elizabeth and Enid ate their lunches quietly, biding their time. They both knew they couldn't afford to rush. When they sprang the trap, they had to catch Kirk the first time; there wouldn't be a second chance.

Finally the moment arrived. Some of the boys had drifted out to the lawn, and others had gone off to get more food. Kirk was alone, leaning back against the window, calmly eating an ice cream sandwich and surveying the cafeteria.

Elizabeth quickly slipped a handful of magazine clippings out of her notebook and passed them across the table. Right on cue, Enid let out a gasp of surprise.

"Liz! You never told me your cousin was so—so gorgeous! I can't believe she's so beautiful!"

Almost imperceptibly, Kirk turned his head to listen, and Elizabeth fought to control a grin of triumph.

"Yes," she admitted, pitching her voice just loud enough to carry to the next table. "When she got her modeling contract, none of us were surprised. She's always been the prettiest member of the family."

"And so sophisticated, too," Enid gushed, holding up the pictures for a better view.

Kirk turned completely around then, and stared at the pictures in front of Enid. Elizabeth noted the alert, eager look in his eyes, but she kept her own expression impassive. "Well, she does live in New York, after all. Sixteen in Manhattan is a lot more mature than sixteen in Sweet Valley."

"Boy, I'll say." Enid shook her head. "Erica must be one of the most glamorous girls in the country."

Elizabeth let out a tinkling laugh. "Well, you'll get to judge for yourself when she gets here. She's got a screen test in L.A., so she'll be coming up to visit us over the weekend."

"This weekend?"

"No, next."

Kirk was practically hanging over Enid's shoulder to look at the pictures, and Enid suppressed the laughter building up inside her. "Hey," she exclaimed, "that's the weekend of the Swing Fling!"

"Who is that?" said Kirk. He was obviously doing his best to sound casual as he pulled his chair around. He reached for the magazine clippings and spread them out in front of him on the table.

"That's my cousin, Erica Hall," Elizabeth explained, her face a picture of honesty. "She's a model," she added.

Kirk nodded carelessly, but his keen blue eyes were glittering with excitement. "Did I hear you say she'd be in town next weekend?"

A cautious look came into Elizabeth's eyes. "Ye-ess," she said hesitantly. "Why?"

"I want to take her to the dance, that's why," he announced, crossing his arms. He tossed his glossy black hair back off his forehead. "She's exactly my type."

"But—but, Kirk, I don't know. . . ." Elizabeth trailed off.

"What do you mean? She'll be here, won't she?"

Elizabeth shrugged slightly. "Well, sure, but it's just that . . . well, Erica never goes out on blind dates. There are so many guys asking her out all the time that she's really picky."

"Well, of course she'd pick me if she met me," Kirk said in an annoyed tone.

"But she won't even get here until that afternoon. She wouldn't have time to meet you." With an anxious glance at Enid, Elizabeth murmured, "She only likes to go out with really good-looking guys. She never takes a chance."

Kirk's mouth opened and shut in indignance. But his natural arrogance buoyed him up again instantly. "Look, Elizabeth. Just send her my picture. That should take care of everything."

He rummaged in his notebook and pulled out a copy of the previous week's *Oracle*. "See, here I am, getting congratulated by the guy I slaughtered at the Big Mesa tennis tournament. That's my best side."

It took all of Elizabeth's willpower to keep from screaming, but whether it was a scream of laughter or outrage she wasn't sure. True, it was a dirty trick they were playing on Kirk, but he deserved it. And his conceited assurance that his photograph would impress sophisticated Erica Hall just underscored how richly he *did* deserve it.

Elizabeth tried to look hopeful as she took the paper from Kirk. "I don't know. I can't promise anything," she warned, holding up one hand. "But I'll send this to Erica. It's totally up to her."

Kirk smiled arrogantly and picked up the pictures of the glamorous model again. "She'll want to go with me, don't worry. Just send her the photo and tell her all about me. She couldn't say no."

"You've got a point there," Enid put in solemnly. She sent Kirk an adoring look and then turned away shyly to stare out the window as he grinned down at her. Kirk couldn't see Enid's face, but Elizabeth could. And the expression in her friend's large green eyes almost made Elizabeth lose control altogether.

She looked thoughtful for a moment. She knew the more she hesitated, the more avid Kirk would be to take Erica Hall to the Swing Fling. "Well— I'll do my best, Kirk."

He pushed himself away from the table and stood up. "Just do what I said and let me know when she says yes, OK?"

"Sure, Kirk," Elizabeth agreed. "I'll let you know as soon as I hear from her."

"Great. Who knows, maybe you and I can even go out sometime." He winked at her and strolled off.

The two girls watched his retreating figure. They were speechless until he disappeared through the glass doors onto the patio.

Finally they turned to each other, and their eyes met for a long, silent moment.

"Boy, if I had any doubts about this, I don't now," Elizabeth said as she gathered up the clippings. "He deserves everything that's coming to him."

Nine

On Wednesday evening Jessica ran to answer the front door. John Karger was taking her out for dessert, and her fingers were crossed behind her back as she reached for the door handle. Her heart gave a thump of excitement and started hammering wildly when she saw him on the doorstep.

"Hi, I'm John Karger. Jessica?"

He had a voice to match his face—perfect. And the rest of him was pretty good, too, Jessica noted with delight: long, lean legs; strong, artistic hands; and a confident, graceful stance. He was just taking off a pair of preppy tortoise-shell glasses that gave him a serious but intriguing look. Dressed conservatively in khakis and a tweed sportcoat, with scuffed brown loafers and an open-necked shirt that showed his tanned throat, he was very collegiate-looking, and to Jessica's eye very, very sexy.

"Hi!" She welcomed him with her most dazzling smile. "It's so nice to meet you. Let me just get my jacket."

As she turned to open the hall closet, Jessica allowed a brief expression of wild elation to flash across her face. Lila would just *die* when she saw John Karger. The contest was as good as won.

"Ready." She smiled.

His warm brown eyes kindled with admiration as he held the car door open for her. "You know," he said as he slid into the driver's seat, "I have to admit you don't look like the type of girl to be writing personal ads."

"And you don't look like the type of guy to be answering them," she countered, sending him a sidelong glance. "But we're all so rushed these days, right? It's so hard to meet people sometimes."

He nodded emphatically. "That's absolutely right, Jessica. But it's hard to tell what kind of person someone is from a personal ad. Anyway," he continued, sending her a swift smile as he made a right turn, "I thought we could go to this little Greek place I know and have a nice long talk with no interruptions. They serve a mean baklava."

"Great," Jessica breathed, "Perfect." There was plenty of time to find out what baklava was, she decided. Right now the most important thing was to concentrate on the chemistry between them. A "nice long talk with no inter-ruptions" sounded a lot more interesting than any Greek dessert.

She relaxed against the seat back and allowed herself a serene smile. Now the contest was starting to look a little more interesting, and maybe it would even start paying off that night!

"Here it is," John announced. He took her arm again as they entered the dimly lit Greek "tavern," and they were soon ensconced in an intimate booth. The haunting strains of Greek folk music played plaintively in the background, and a dark-eyed waitress took their order for baklava.

"This is nice," murmured Jessica, looking deep into John's brown eyes.

He smiled and rested his chin on his hands, returning her penetrating stare. "So tell me about yourself, Jessica. I want to know everything about you."

Another thrill of anticipation rippled through Jessica as she met his steady, intent gaze. "Well, I like lots of things," she began, making little circles on the table with one index finger. "Like having a good time, doing exciting things."

"Like what?"

Jessica considered briefly. "I guess you could say I like a dare. I'll do anything once—and I'll do it again if I like it," she added suggestively.

"I bet you've got tons of guys asking you out all the time."

That was a tricky one, but Jessica decided she knew the best way to handle it. "Well, I do," she admitted with a hint of modesty. "But the problem is, most boys are so immature. I'm hoping to meet someone more adult. . . ."

John certainly seemed adult, in her opinion. His steady, serious eyes were startlingly intense, and he seemed genuinely interested in her—who she was and what her thoughts were. Smiling faintly, Jessica decided he even seemed enthralled.

"But what about you?" she prodded. "Tell me about yourself."

He shrugged and swept a lock of honey-gold hair out of his eyes with a careless, unconscious gesture. "Oh, I'm just another guy. I'm a freshman—a sociology major. That's all."

"Sociology? What's that all about?"

His eyes were steady on hers as he said, "People. I study people."

"I see." Jessica thought she certainly did see. John was certainly studying *her* intently!

"Would you consider yourself an adventure-seeker, Jessica?"

"Yes. You could definitely say that."

"Give me an example," he urged, a gleam of admiration in his romantic brown eyes.

Jessica laughed. "Well, there was the time I made Jeremy Frank have me on his TV show, and the time I got stuck in a cave with a bear. And once I smuggled a puppy into our house and kept him hidden from my parents for a whole week. I've done all kinds of things like that. . . ."

As John continued to ask her questions, Jessica couldn't help making a series of mental notes. He seemed like the serious, almost studious, type, but in an intense, exciting way, not boring or dull. She instantly decided that she liked the serious type. And furthermore, he seemed to be utterly fascinated by her, which really wasn't surprising, Jessica admitted to herself. Yes, she had definitely made a conquest, and one of her most gratifying conquests ever!

She took another bite of the sticky-sweet baklava, a nut-filled pastry drenched in honey, and smiled at John, giving him her most alluring smile. She delicately licked a morsel of pastry from her lower lip.

"You know, Jessica, I've read a lot of personal ads, but yours was really striking. I mean, you know what you want, and you just go for it. I like that."

"Oh, John," she whispered. "I think we've got a lot in common."

He smiled and took a sip of his coffee. "You really think so?"

"Mmm."

For a moment he continued to stare into her eyes, but then he sighed and glanced at his watch. "I'm really sorry, Jessica, but I'm going to have to take you home now."

Jessica's face fell. "But it's so early!"

"I know, but I've got a lot of studying to do tonight. I'm really sorry I have to cut this short," he repeated, a little wistfully.

"Well, maybe we could—see each other again," she suggested, giving him her most charming smile.

"I'd love to. I really enjoyed meeting you, Jessica. Let me think. Tomorrow I'm busy, and Friday. But maybe over the weekend some time. Can I call you?"

Hiding her disappointment, Jessica nodded. "Of course, John. Please call."

"Great. Let's get you home now."

The ride back to Jessica's house was interspersed with more intent, probing questions from John, and Jessica felt a glow of elation. It was obvious that he couldn't get enough of her. When the car finally pulled to a stop in front of her house, she turned her face to him, certain that he would kiss her good night.

"I had a wonderful time," she murmured, her voice husky. She waited for his lips to touch hers.

But nothing happened. He just smiled his gorgeous smile again. "Me too, Jessica. Good night."

Apparently John Karger was a gentleman. Maybe that was part of his serious attitude. *Well, all in good time*, Jessica told herself as she let herself out of the car. She watched as he drove away, then floated dreamily up the steps to the door.

What a triumph, she marveled. Who would have thought a personal ad would attract such a hunk? Closing her eyes briefly, Jessica relived some of the most intense moments of the evening and decided with satisfaction that she was definitely in love.

Penny put down her book and stared off into space. As good as *Huckleberry Finn* was, she found herself reading the same paragraph over and over.

Her wandering gaze came to rest on the envelope on her desk. Lynne had given it to her that afternoon, but she hadn't read it yet. It was from Jamie, Penny was sure. But she hadn't been able to bring herself to open it before, and risk opening up all the hurt and disappointment she felt inside.

Now she knew she had to read it. There was no way to ignore it.

With a calm that surprised her, Penny slit open the envelope and extracted the letter. Her eyes ran down the page quickly. Then she re-read it, trying hard to quell the rising feeling of hope.

Could it really have been an unforeseen emergency that had kept him away on Friday afternoon? If so, maybe there was still hope.

Then the doubts came rushing back in. What if—it was horrible even to consider it—he stood her up *again*? She didn't think she'd be able to handle that. Just thinking about it almost made her vow not to take that chance.

But she read the letter for a third time. Jamie's words did ring with sincerity. It *couldn't* be fake. It just couldn't be.

Penny drew a deep breath. Foolish or not, she felt she had to trust him, give him the second chance he asked for so earnestly. Because even though it seemed like a risk, the reward could be wonderful. By four o'clock the next afternoon, she would know once and for all.

"OK, Jamie," she whispered aloud. "I'll be there."

Neil paced back and forth in front of his car at the Dairi Burger parking lot. Suddenly he felt an overwhelming shyness. What was he going to say to her? He wanted to find that magic combination of words that would make everything clear, and at the same time make her realize what a perfect match they were.

A chilling thought stopped him: What if she was disappointed to find that Jamie was really just Neil Freemount? Would she be expecting an ace student like herself?

He swallowed hard. Up until then, Neil realized, Kirk's arrogance had rubbed off on him and made him take for granted that Penny would be happy to know he was "Jamie." Now he wasn't so confident. After all, he wasn't a particularly distinguished student. His grades were decent, and he knew he was an impressive tennis player, but would that be enough for Penny? He had a much higher opinion of *her* than he had of himself.

And what *would* he say to her, after all? Should he explain what really happened last Friday, that he was too afraid to stand up to Kirk and the others? Or should he just stick to his excuse about an emergency? Probably that was the best course of action. He didn't want Penny to think badly of him.

A car pulled up into a nearby parking space, and he nearly jumped out of his skin when Penny stepped out of the car. He watched, hypnotized, as she pocketed her keys and walked to the front entrance of the Dairi Burger to wait—for him.

As he stood there, squaring his shoulders and getting ready to follow her, another car pulled into the lot and honked at him. He turned with a sinking heart to see a white Trans Am slide into a parking space. The doors banged shut, and Kirk and Michael sauntered over to him.

"Hey, Freemount. What's up?" Kirk asked.

"Nothing."

Kirk's eyebrows shot up in an ironic expression. "Waiting for someone? Or shouldn't we ask?"

Michael Harris chuckled and kicked at a stone. The three boys watched as it skittered across the pavement and landed directly in front of the entrance of the Dairi Burger. Standing there in plain view was Penny Ayala.

Kirk turned quickly to face Neil, who felt his cheeks reddening. "You're not meeting *her*, are you?"

Neil cursed himself silently for hesitating so long, and he felt his hands start to sweat. If he admitted he was meeting Penny, that would definitely be the end of his association with Kirk Anderson. With a pang of nostalgia, Neil remembered that feeling of belonging, of being admired.

And then he remembered the feeling in English class on Tuesday when it looked as though Penny admired him, too. He rubbed his hands on his jeans and glanced at the entrance. Penny was still there, but she had a worried frown on her face. It was ten after four. He was *not* going to stand her up again.

He met Kirk's eyes steadily. "Yes, as a matter of fact, I *am* meeting Penny. Do you have anything to say about that, Kirk?"

His voice was strong and assured, and his determination seemed to impress the other boys. But Kirk still stood offensively in front of Neil, his arms crossed and an expression of bullying humor on his face. "Are you serious? Give me a break!"

For a long, tense moment, they stared at each other. It was a battle of wills between Kirk and Neil, and finally Neil let out a short, ironic laugh. "Give it up, Anderson. I really don't care what you think of me anymore."

Kirk pulled his head back quickly, as if he couldn't believe what he had just heard. He and Michael exchanged a brief glance, and then Kirk shrugged. "No problem."

A flood of relief and pride filled Neil, a feeling he had never known before. He knew instinctively that he had just won, had just done something *right*.

"OK," he said lightly. "See you later."

And with that he walked across the parking lot to meet Penny.

Ten

Penny stood rigid on the sidewalk, her heart pounding with anger and mortification. If this was Jamie's idea of a joke, he had a pretty sick sense of humor, she thought, alternating between fury and pain, and trembling with the effort to stay calm.

How could I have misjudged him so badly?

She drew a long, shaky breath to steady herself, turned to the parking lot, and ran smack into Neil Freemount.

"Sorry!" he exclaimed. His face turned a bright crimson, which startled Penny. There was no reason for him to be *that* embarrassed. "I—I—"

"Hi, Neil. It's OK, don't worry about it. Excuse me." She tried to walk by him, but he stepped in front of her, trying to speak.

"Penny, I—"

"Neil, what is it? I really have to go. I'm

114

meeting someone." Her own face reddened. She *had* been meeting someone, but not anymore.

"I know."

She frowned, puzzled. "What?"

"Penny, I'm Jamie," he blurted out. He looked at her, his gaze level and serious as he drew a deep breath and smiled at her. "I'm really sorry I was late."

Speechless with surprise, Penny gaped at him. Her mind was a total blank.

Suddenly Neil chuckled. "Don't look so shocked. It really was just plain old me all along."

"Oh! I didn't mean—I mean I'm not *upset*—" Breaking off, Penny looked into his laughing brown eyes and felt herself smiling. Then she laughed.

"You're not sorry, are you? I mean, I'm probably not the sort of guy you expected."

Sorry? How could she possibly be sorry that Jamie had turned out to be handsome Neil Freemount? And there was obviously a lot more to him than just good looks and a friendly, easy-going manner. His letters had made that clear enough. No, she wasn't sorry. Far from it. She just couldn't believe it, that was all.

"No," she murmured, and shook her head. "I'm very pleased to meet you, Jamie. Finally."

A cloud flickered across Neil's face for an instant. He looked suddenly anxious and worried in spite of his smile. "Listen, how about we go inside for a soda or something, OK?"

Penny nodded, wondering nervously what had put that hint of reserve in his voice. They quickly ordered sodas at the counter, then found an empty booth.

For a moment neither of them spoke. They just looked at each other, totally isolated and oblivious to the noisy after-school crowd that jammed the Dairi Burger. Video games buzzed and bleeped, girls called to each other, and boys formed tight, conspiratorial huddles around tables. But Penny and Neil's booth was an island. Neither was aware of anything else.

Then Neil broke the silence, his voice low. "Penny, I wasn't going to tell you this, but I don't want to lie to you. I have too much respect for you not to be totally up front about this. On Friday—I was there."

A hot blush washed over Penny's face, but she tried to keep her voice calm and noncommittal. "Oh?"

"Yeah, you see . . . dammit, Penny! I hate to tell you this, but it all started as a joke. Some guys on the tennis team saw your ad and decided to write back as a group."

Penny's heart gave a sickening lurch. *A joke. It was a joke.* She stared at the scratched Formica tabletop, trying to form a coherent thought.

Neil cleared his throat. "But when you started answering the letters, it wasn't a joke anymore, Penny. I really wanted to know who you were, but it was still just a game for the others. I didn't know what to do!"

She looked up finally and met his eyes. "And Friday?" she asked tonelessly.

Neil looked away from her bleak gaze. But then he looked at her squarely. "I can't excuse what I did, Penny. When they all saw it was you, they said you were too serious and—"

"I can just imagine." Penny had a sour taste in her mouth. She could imagine all too well what the boys must have said when they saw her. Penny Ayala was obviously nobody's idea of a date.

For a moment there was a heavy silence.

"I've never regretted anything more," Neil continued at last. "I have never been so ashamed of myself as when I let those guys do my thinking for me." His voice quivered with intensity, and his hands were clenched together, the knuckles white.

"I'm really sorry," he added.

Penny drew a long breath. "Well, now that you've apologized, I guess I'll go while I still have a little bit of my dignity left."

"Penny, please!" He grabbed her hand as she tried to get up and looked at her imploringly. "Please. I didn't just come here to apologize. I want—I want to . . ."

Slowly Penny dropped her eyes from his steady, intense gaze and looked at the hand that clasped hers so tightly. It was warm and

117

strong, and she could almost feel the emotion running through him and up into her arm and all through her body.

"You really mean it, don't you?" she wondered aloud, shaking her head slowly from side to side.

A harsh laugh escaped him. "I really do. I really thought we had something in our letters, and I was hoping it could be the same in person. But if you don't even want to talk to me at all, I wouldn't blame you."

Penny felt herself smile in spite of herself. "I think I could bear to talk to you, Neil."

He returned her smile. "You think so?"

"Yes."

He let out a deep sigh of relief. "Do you think you could bear to go to the Swing Fling next weekend? With me, I mean?"

Penny made a face that looked as though she were debating seriously whether or not she could. "Well, it would be hard, but I guess I could manage it."

Neil laughed out loud. "Don't worry. I'm not really so obnoxious. You might even learn to like me one of these years."

Holding her breath, Penny met his warm, gentle eyes again. She didn't trust herself to speak, but she had learned to like him already, especially his honesty, his sensitivity. And suddenly she realized how much of an effort it must have been for him to stand up to his friends the way he had. There was a lot more to Neil Freemount than met the eye, and she knew she would enjoy getting to know him.

He seemed to sense her difficulty in answering him. He cocked his head to one side and squeezed her hand, giving her a gentle smile. "And there's a free concert on the beach that Saturday afternoon. It's really informal—just a lot of people hanging out, having a good time. We could go to that, have a picnic, and then go to the dance. What do you say?"

"What do I say? *Yes!*" Leaning forward across the table, she said, "I'd love to, Neil Freemount."

Without warning, he leaned forward also and kissed her quickly. "Me, too," he said, a smile dancing in his eyes. "Me, too."

"Did you see that?"

Jessica and Lila looked up from the magazine they had been poring over together. Cara Walker was looking across the Dairi Burger with an expression of surprise on her face.

"What?" asked Jessica.

"Neil Freemount and Penny Ayala over there. They just kissed."

Jessica craned her neck. "You're kidding!"

"I swear, sometimes you see the most unbelievable couples," Lila drawled, jiggling the ice in her soda cup. "Hey, Maria, can you get me an order of fries while you're up there," she called as Maria Santelli walked past them.

"Speaking of couples . . ." Jessica cut in

quickly. She left her sentence unfinished, relishing the expectant looks on her best friends' faces.

Cara gave her a lopsided smile. Long friendship had made them all used to each other's habits by now, and Jessica's theatricality was well known to Cara and Lila. "Yessss, Jessica? *Speaking* of couples'?"

"There just happens to be a new couple, and I'm not talking about Penny and Neil." Jessica tossing her blond hair back over her shoulder.

Lila shot her a keen glance. "Oh, really? Does this have anything to do with our little wager?"

"What wager?" Cara asked eagerly.

Turning to Cara, Jessica explained, "Lila and I both placed personal ads to see who could come up with the best guys that way. And I won."

"You won!" Lila snapped. "Who says you won?"

Jessica lowered her eyes in an attempt at modesty. "Well, last night I had a date with one of the guys who answered my ad," she said. "And let's just say he was—unbelievable." She grinned at them, enjoying the effect she was having.

"What was he like, Jess?" Cara asked breathlessly, her brown eyes alight with excitement. "What's his name?"

For a moment Jessica considered telling them all about John and his obvious and flattering fascination with her. But she decided to hold back. It was more fun, and made him slightly mysterious.

Just then Maria came back with a dish heaped with french fries. "At your service,' she said, smiling.

Lila paid her. As Maria walked back to her own table where Winston was sitting, Jessica helped herself to Lila's fries. With a french fry poised in the air, she announced, "Well—all I'm going to tell you now is that he's gorgeous, and he's crazy about me."

Lila chuckled, as if she knew something Jessica didn't. "Gorgeous, huh? Well, Jessica, I just happen to have a date tonight, with someone I think will win our little contest. So don't speak too soon."

"Well, how are you going to decide who wins?" Cara demanded, looking from Jessica to Lila.

Jessica frowned. "Good question. I guess we never really decided that, did we?"

"I have an idea," Cara went on. "Both of you bring your dates to the Swing Fling, and then you can see who won."

"Cara, I already have a date for the Swing Fling," Lila said.

"Besides," Jessica added, "my date is in college. He would never go to some juvenile high school dance."

Cara laughed. "Oh, come on, Jessica. Steven is in college, and he likes to go to our dances."

Jessica hid a smile. Without question her brother was terrific. But in her opinion he was nowhere *near* John Karger's league. She put her hand on Cara's arm condescendingly. "I know; isn't he sweet?"

With an ironic smile, Cara pulled her arm away. "Yes, he is. I'll tell him you said so," she added.

"Truce, truce!" Lila cut in. "Anyway, my date is in college, too, and believe me, he's very sophisticated. I know that already, just from his letter. Now Steve is a very nice guy, and I'm sure your little friend is nice, too," she added condescendingly, grinning at Jessica. "But I'm talking about a real *man*. I think we'll see that my date is the winner."

Jessica picked up her soda and took a long sip. Lila could really drive her crazy sometimes. Finally she was composed enough to say, "Well, we'll just see, Lila. We'll just see."

Elizabeth pulled the Fiat up to the curb in front of the Dairi Burger. A glance at her watch told her it was five-thirty. Jessica should be coming out any minute. That is, if her twin remembered to look at the time.

She picked up her notebook and reread her notes for her next "Eyes and Ears" column. The personal ad project had already yielded results, and there were some new couples to mention. She glanced up to see if Jessica was coming, and saw Penny and Neil, deep in conversation, walking out the front door.

"Well good for you, Penny," she said softly, shaking her head. With a little chuckle she jotted down the initials, P.A. and N.F. on her list.

"Hey, Liz!"

Turning around, Elizabeth noted with dismay that Kirk Anderson was striding toward her. She controlled her expression as he leaned against the side of the convertible and looked down at her.

"So, did you do like I said?"

Smiling sweetly, Elizabeth reassured him. "Yes, Kirk. I sent your picture and a letter to Erica yesterday. But you really shouldn't get your hopes up. There's no guarantee she'll say yes."

He raised one eyebrow. "She's the one who should be getting her hopes up, Liz. Don't worry about me."

With that he sauntered off to join Michael Harris. Elizabeth stared after him. *We'll see about that, Kirk,* she said to herself.

A momentary pang of guilt about lying washed over her. But when she remembered the pain Kirk had inflicted on Penny—and the conceited pride he took in doing it—she steeled herself against feeling sorry for him. Kirk Anderson didn't deserve any remorse from her. Not one bit.

Eleven

"Jessica, what made you write that personal ad?"

"Hmm?" she said dreamily, lost in John Karger's romantic brown eyes. "What did you say?"

The university snack bar was packed with students that cloudy Sunday afternoon, but to Jessica it seemed an intimate spot just for two. John leaned back in his chair, rubbing his chin thoughtfully as he looked at her. "What really made you decide to write a personal ad, Jessica?"

"Does it matter now?" she asked. What difference did it make, now that she had him?

He chuckled. "Yes, it does matter to me. I told you before—I never expected to find a girl like you writing one."

Jessica snapped out of her dreamy contemplation. It didn't seem exactly diplomatic to admit it was to win a bet with her best friend. But what reason could she give that would sound good? She sure wasn't one of the lonely-heart drabs who usually resorted to them.

"Well, let's just say I wanted to see what would happen," she said truthfully, swirling the ice around in her cup.

"That's what I thought. Another one of your adventures, right?"

"Mmm. Yes, that's right," Jessica admitted with a grin. That seemed to be one of the characteristics he liked the most about her. She was perfectly willing to let him think she would hijack an airplane if it kept him hanging on her every word the way he did. Now on their second date, John was still displaying an almost obsessive interest in her, asking questions, urging her to talk about herself. And since there were few things Jessica enjoyed discussing as much as herself, she was more than happy to oblige. Especially with such a receptive, and gorgeous, audience.

Lila's arch smile on Friday morning came back to her. Apparently Lila's date on Thursday night had been pretty hot, but Jessica was confident that he couldn't be as wonderful as John. Lila had chosen to be just as secretive as Jessica had: They both simply refused to go into details before they could judge each other's dates for themselves. They had just agreed to think of some way for the four of them to get together.

Of course, they had to be subtle enough so that the two boys didn't know they were being compared like prize livestock.

Just then Jessica had an idea. "John," she murmured, looking up at him with a melting smile. "I'd really like for you to meet my best friend. There's a dance next Saturday night. . . ." Her voice trailed off, a hopeful gleam lighting her blue-green eyes.

"Well, I'm busy next Saturday night, I'm afraid. I'm working on a big sociology project with my partner. But I'd like to meet your friend, Jessica. I know—there's a free concert at the Sweet Valley beach that afternoon. There'll be a couple of bands, food, people just hanging out, you know? I'm going with some friends. Will you be there?"

"If you are."

He smiled. "You flatter me, Jessica. Look, why don't I meet you and your friend there, OK?"

Jessica took a long pull on her soda straw. He might *think* he was going to be busy that night. But Jessica had other plans for him. Once she found him at the beach, she'd make certain he didn't want to leave her side for an instant. He would be busy all right, but with her. It was time for the studious John Karger to learn something about romance. His sociology partner would just have to find some other way to spend his Saturday night.

"That would be fine, John."

"Great. Now I've really got to get to the library, or I can kiss my grade-point average goodbye. I'll see you next Saturday, OK?"

Jessica regretfully stood up with him and dragged herself across campus to her car. But as she drove the convertible back to Sweet Valley, the warm ocean breeze whipping through her hair, her optimism returned. John was hooked, there was no question about that. Just why he kept cutting their dates short to hit the books was beyond her, but she put it down to his serious nature. Still, she had supreme confidence in her ability to change all that. And the leopard-spotted bikini she had seen at Lisette's the other day would be the first course in John's reeducation.

In spite of the overcast sky—a rarity in Sweet Valley—Elizabeth and Enid were in their bathing suits on the Wakefields' patio. A light breeze stirred up little waves in the water, and they slapped gently against the sides of the pool.

"I don't know about this, Enid. I'm suddenly not so sure we should go ahead with it." Elizabeth tucked her feet up under her on the chaise and stared moodily into the water. Whenever she came into contact with Kirk's abrasive and infuriating personality, her resolve was steady.

But when she was alone and had time to think about it, she felt terribly guilty.

Enid sighed faintly. "I know what you mean. If it were anyone else, I'd say we should forget it." She paused, then grinned. "But the way I see it, our little surprise won't even phase him. Don't worry."

"You're probably right. Besides, even though it's nice to forgive and forget, revenge *is* sweet, isn't it?"

They shared a guilty smile and then Elizabeth pushed herself up from her comfortable pose. "Well, I guess it's time to put Phase Two into action." Enid followed Elizabeth into the house.

As Elizabeth picked up the phone in the kitchen and dialed directory assistance, Enid chuckled softly. "You know, with that sneaky look in your eyes, suddenly you look just like Jessica!"

"Did I hear my name?" came Jessica's voice. She pushed open the kitchen door. "Who looks like me?"

Her twin laughed. "Well, some people think I do, as a matter of fact. But I guess I was looking especially devious, which makes me look even more like you." She couldn't help laughing at Jessica's expression.

"Devious, huh? I think I'll let that one slide. I'm in too good a mood to let you spoil it. But what's to be devious about?"

Dialing the Andersons' phone number, Elizabeth said, "Calling Kirk to say Erica is wild to meet him."

"Oooh, great," squealed Jessica. "I'm glad I got back in time. What are you going to say?"

But the phone was ringing at Kirk's end, and Enid held up one hand for silence, watching Elizabeth's face intently. Elizabeth winked at them.

"Hello?" came Kirk's voice through the receiver.

"Hi, Kirk. I'm glad I caught you. This is Elizabeth Wakefield."

"Yeah?"

"My cousin Erica called me last night from New York. She got my letter yesterday with your picture—"

"What did she say?"

Elizabeth winced. Even Kirk's telephone manner was all arrogance. "She said yes, she'll go to the Swing Fling with you. She'd like to meet you."

Kirk chuckled knowingly. "What did I tell you? Tell her I'll pick her up at your place at eight, OK?"

"Well, you can't do that," Elizabeth explained hastily. She wrapped the phone cord around one finger as she went on. "See, she's driving up from L.A. that afternoon and will only be getting here just in time. She'd rather just meet you outside the gym."

"That's fine with me."

"Kirk, I really don't think you should take her."

"Why not?" It was almost a snarl, and Elizabeth rolled her eyes at Enid and Jessica, who were trying to get close enough to the earpiece to hear what Kirk was saying.

Elizabeth drew a deep breath. "It's just that I don't think you'd like her, Kirk. She's really arrogant and conceited about her looks—she's always bragging about how wonderful she is." *Just like you*, she added silently.

He laughed. "I like a girl with self-confidence," he said smoothly. "If she's got it, she should flaunt it. I like that."

Elizabeth gritted her teeth. "She's just impossible to have fun with, Kirk. She's so self-centered, so bossy, so superior—"

"Look, I don't know what your problem is. All of a sudden you don't want me going out with your cousin. But I'm taking her out, got it?"

"Well, all right. You'd better get her an orchid or something really fancy as a corsage. She's used to being treated well."

"I will, I will. Thanks, Liz."

" 'Bye, Kirk." Slowly Elizabeth hung up the phone, then stared at it for a moment. When she turned to the others, her expression was one of utter amazement.

"Well?" Jessica demanded. "I couldn't hear a word he said."

"Me, neither," said Enid.

Drawing a deep breath, Elizabeth shook her head in disgust. "He was practically drooling into the phone. How can he not have realized I was describing himself?"

"Well, he obviously loves himself, right?" Enid commented dryly. "So it makes sense he'd like a girl who's just like him."

"Well anyway, we've got him right where we want him," Elizabeth said. "Now all we can do is wait until Saturday."

Twelve

Elizabeth sat down under her favorite tree on the front lawn at school and eagerly opened up the new *Oracle*. Munching contentedly on a tuna sandwich, she read her own column.

The Eyes and Ears of Sweet Valley High have been tuned in over the past couple of weeks to find out what results the new personal ads have had. Results have been promising, to say the least. The course of true love has run straight and swift through the mail, so you can count on seeing some new couples on the dance floor at Saturday night's Swing Fling. Keep your eyes on tennis players and newspaper editors in particular. . . .

"Somebody might get the wrong idea and

think you're conceited or something," Jeffrey said with a grin.

She looked up quickly. "It's a sin all reporters share, you know. We just can't get enough of our own writing."

Jeffrey edged himself a little closer to her and gently pushed a strand of hair out of her eyes. "Want to know what my opinion is?" he said huskily.

"Mmm . . . opinion about what?" she shot back, her eyes dancing.

He suddenly looked very serious. "The state of affairs in the Far East, of course. What else could I be talking about?"

"You rat!" Elizabeth put her hands around his throat and pretended to throttle him. But he pulled her hands away and wrapped them around his neck, drawing her closer.

"Ever been kissed by a rat?" he teased.

"Hi, Liz. Hi, Jeffrey. Can we sit with you?"

They looked up, smiling, to see Aaron Dallas, Jeffrey's best friend, and Heather Sanford. "Of course! Pull up a chair—or a lawn."

Heather grinned and smoothed her buff-colored linen skirt as she sat down. She was always exquisitely dressed, and most of her outfits were of her own design. "I read your column this morning," she said, a gleeful smile lighting her soft brown eyes. "But it's not fair to be so mysterious, you know. Who got matched up?"

"Oh, you'll find out soon enough," Elizabeth said nonchalantly. Then she giggled. "I was talking mainly about Penny Ayala and Neil Freemount. It turns out they have a lot in common, but they were both too shy to get together until now. Isn't that great?"

"Mmm."

Aaron lay back on the grass, twirling a leaf stem in his fingers. "Hey, Liz. I never knew you had a cousin in New York who's a model. You've kept her a big secret."

"What! You do?" Heather's eyes grew round with surprise.

Rolling over onto his side, Aaron propped himself up on his elbow. "Yeah, this morning in the locker room before gym, Kirk Anderson was talking about how she's coming to Sweet Valley just to go to the dance with him on Saturday night. Everybody's talking about it now."

Elizabeth felt her lips quiver, and she met Jeffrey's eyes steadily. "He said that, huh?"

"Yeah. He says you sent her his picture and she just can't wait to meet him. He says she's really gorgeous. What's her name—Erica something? Hall?"

"Not Erica Hall!" Heather gasped, turning to stare at Elizabeth. "She's your *cousin*? You've got to be kidding! She's just the most beautiful model in the world."

Elizabeth looked at her two friends in silence

for a moment. "Listen, I'm going to tell you something, but you've got to swear not to tell a soul. Promise?"

They nodded, awed by her seriousness. Aaron glanced at Jeffrey, who grinned back at him silently.

Elizabeth popped the last morsel of her sandwich into her mouth and wiped her hands on a paper napkin. "OK. Now this is strictly confidential. . . ."

Jessica snapped open *The Oracle* to her twin's column and took a bite of her ice cream sandwich. She never admitted it, but she always read "Eyes and Ears" first and was still proud of her sister's talent. The column was all about the personal ads, and Jessica repressed a grin, thinking about who had responded to *her* ad.

She glanced up as Lila sat down with her and Cara. Across the noisy cafeteria, Amy Sutton spotted them and waved, then began weaving toward them through the tables.

"Did you read about who's going out now because of those dumb ads?" Amy said, popping open a can of diet soda and nodding at Jessica's copy of the paper. "If you ask me, I don't think anybody worth dating really needs to use those things."

"I wouldn't be too sure about that if I were you," Lila said. She tossed her light brown hair

135

back over her shoulders and leaned forward on her elbows. "*I* happen to have written one of those dumb ads, Amy. And let me tell you, the guy I met would drive you out of your mind with jealousy."

Amy's blue eyes widened with amazement. "You're kidding!"

"Nope. So did Jessica. Except—well, I don't want to hurt her feelings, but . . ."

Cara giggled as Sandra Bacon and Jean West sat down to join them. "You two haven't heard about their bet, have you?"

All eyes turned to Jessica and Lila. "What bet?" Sandra asked, obviously intrigued.

Jessica shrugged. "Lila and I had a little discussion about the best way to write a personal ad to get the kind of guy you want. So we each placed an ad, and we're going to see who got the best date out of it."

Everyone laughed. "I don't believe it!" Jean gasped, biting her lower lip and shaking her head. "Not even you two would do something like that."

"Believe it," Lila said crisply. "And believe this, too: I won."

"Who says you won?" Jessica cried. She glared at Lila, fed up with her friend's arrogance.

"Yeah, who says?" added Cara, coming to Jessica's defense. "You haven't met each others' dates yet, have you?"

Jessica shook her head vehemently. "No. But

my date is meeting me at that free concert at the beach on Saturday, so I suggest you bring yours, Lila. Then we'll settle this once and for all."

"Good idea," Amy said. "And the rest of us can be the judges!"

"Right," said Cara. "I think that's a great idea. Now what we need to do—"

But Jessica and Lila were furious. "Hold on a minute," Jessica commanded. "How did you all get in on this?"

Cara shrugged. "Look, it's obvious neither one of you would ever admit the guy you got wasn't the best, so how can you come to a fair decision about who won? You need someone else there to make that decision for you."

Nodding vigorously, Sandra added, "That's right. I think the four of us should go and be the impartial judges."

Jessica met Lila's eyes steadily. "It's OK with me if it's OK with Lila."

"I've got nothing to worry about," Lila said disdainfully. "Because there's no doubt in my mind that I'm going to win. I would have given Liz a scoop, but really, the relationship we have is already too personal for the press."

With a snort, Jessica licked the ice cream from between the sides of her ice cream sandwich. Let Lila keep thinking that, if she wanted to. Jessica could afford to be generous and give Lila her moment of deluded happiness. It would be brief enough, anyway.

"Whatever you say, Lila," she said sweetly. She turned to Cara, Sandra, Jean, and Amy. "The concert starts at four, so why don't we all meet by the lifeguard station at three-fifteen. That should give us all time to rendezvous."

"Hey, what if it's an even split—two to two?" Sandra asked.

"We can get Maria to come," Amy put in, her eyes dancing with eagerness. "Boy, this is going to be great. The battle of the blind dates. But wait a minute. What are the stakes? I mean, what does the winner win?"

Jessica squirmed in her seat. "We didn't bet money. We didn't bet anything. It's just a matter of principle to see who's right."

"But that's so boring!" Cara said, tapping her chin with one finger. "Let's think of something to spice it up a little."

"How about whoever wins takes her date to the Swing Fling," suggested Lila, grinning fiendishly at Jessica. "And the loser has to go *alone*."

Jessica stared at Lila and then burst out laughing. "Ok with me, Lila. But you're just setting yourself up."

Amy crossed her arms. "Let us be the judge of that, Jessica."

Thirteen

"That's some bathing suit, Jess."

Jessica flashed her mother a broad smile. "Like it?"

'Hmm. I think I'd like it a little better on someone else's daughter," Mrs. Wakefield replied as she sat down at the kitchen table. "But it certainly is a knockout. Have a good time at the concert, sweetie."

Jessica slipped her arms into a filmy beach cover-up. The new leopard-spotted bikini showed alluringly through the sheer fabric, an effect Jessica was more than pleased with. She kissed her mother on the cheek. "I will, Mom. I will."

"Is Liz going with you?"

"Jeffrey's picking her up. Got to run, Mom!"

Minutes later Jessica was maneuvering the red Fiat Spider into a parking space in the lot at the beach. The pavement was oven hot through her sandals as she stepped out of the car, and Jessica curled her toes under the gold straps. It was a gloriously sunny afternoon, and the beach was already packed with groups of people sitting around on blankets or playing volleyball.

Jessica angled the side mirror up to check her appearance and gave her reflection a wink. Studious John Karger had seen the last of his books and his stupid old sociology project. The cover-up was off in a flash. "Look out, Johnny boy. Look out."

Everything was ready. She had called her date for the Swing Fling, Jim Daley, and canceled with a glib excuse. When she entered the gym that night, she would be with John Karger. There was no doubt about it in Jessica's mind.

"Jessica, over here!"

The shout came from beyond the lifeguard station, and Jessica caught a glimpse of Amy, Cara, and Maria among the crowd. Rock music began pulsating in the tangy breeze, and Jessica felt herself grow more and more excited as she made her way toward her friends. This was going to be the moment of truth!

"Where's your mystery man?" Cara asked, her dark eyes gleaming.

Jessica craned her neck to check out the crowd. Already she could see dozens of Sweet Valley High students milling around. But John Karger was nowhere in sight. "He's meeting me here. Don't worry."

Amy nudged her elbow. "Look, here comes Lila."

As Lila approached, Jessica's expression grew stormy and her eyes flashed. An oversize designer T-shirt was knotted above Lila's left hip, revealing the bottom half of a leopard-spotted bikini.

"Nice suit," Lila said grimly, joining them. "I guess after years of being a twin, it's just natural for you to copy."

"*I'm* not copying you!" Jessica glared angrily at her friend. "*You're* the one who's copying me!"

"Hold it, you two! Give me a break!"

Amy pushed herself between them, then crossed her arms. "We're not judging your bathing suits, remember We're here to see who got the best results from her personal ad. Where's your date, Lila?" she continued as Jean and Sandra ran up.

"John's meeting me here," Lila snapped, turning to face Amy.

Jessica's head jerked back. "John? His name is John?"

"Yeah. What's wrong with that? Oh! There he is!" Lila waved at someone in the crowd, then broke into a run. Amy, Maria, Sandra, and Jean quickly followed her.

"What is it, Jess?" Cara asked, noting her strange expression.

"My date's named John, too."

Cara shrugged. "So what? It's the most common name in the world."

They followed in the direction the other girls had gone, and Jessica felt a peculiar sensation settling into the pit of her stomach. Up ahead she could see a group of girls milling around a tall boy. The sensation began to get even stronger.

"Who do you think all those girls are?" she whispered as they drew closer. Girls of all types and sizes were clamoring around the still-hidden boy, and Lila was standing on the outskirts of the group, her face chalky white. A gap opened up in the crowd, and Jessica met John Karger's gaze with a shocked gasp.

"Hey, Jessica!" John shouted happily. "Hi." Standing next to him was a stunning redhead. "Girls, this is Faye, my partner on my sociology project. And my girlfriend," he added, giving Faye an adoring smile.

Stunned speechless, Jessica stared at Lila, whose jaw was clenched in anger. Their eyes met, and Jessica raised her eyebrows as high as they would go. Had they both been dating the same guy? And for that matter, had all these other girls been dating him, too?

"Just *what* is going on here?" a pudgy blond girl choked out. "I thought we had a date, John!"

"What? He has a date with me!" another girl exclaimed indignantly.

Faye shook her head with an amused chuckle. "I'm afraid you're both wrong."

But John appeared concerned, "I'm sorry, I hope I didn't give you the impression—"

"What are you trying to say?" came another indignant voice.

"I was doing research for my sociology project."

"Research!" echoed an infuriated brunette.

He nodded emphatically, his face lighting with eagerness. "Yes. You see, I wanted to see how people presented themselves in personal ads, and what they thought was appealing about themselves, so I answered all of your ads."

Jessica gulped. He answered ads regardless of what they said?

One girl let out a wail. "But, John! I thought you really liked me!"

He turned crimson and began stammering. Apparently the serious-minded John Karger wasn't aware of the effects of his flattering, probing questions—or the effects of his romantic brown eyes. "I never meant—I hope you didn't think . . ." His voice trailed off, and he stared back mutely at all the pairs of angry, humiliated eyes focused on him. He swallowed audibly. "Oh, no."

Jessica groaned. "Oh, brother."

Faye let out a peal of laughter. "I knew this would happen, John. I told you!"

At that, all of the girls except the Sweet Valley High contingent turned and stalked away. John smiled feebly at Lila and Jessica. "Do you two, uh . . . know each other?"

Stony silence met this question. A short burst of giggles from the other girls was quickly cut off.

"Well, isn't that a coincidence?" Jessica sneered, shaking her head in disgust.

John looked at Faye, and then off into the distance. "Uh, I think I see someone I know. Come on, Faye." He grabbed his girlfriend by the hand and towed her off.

Finally a torrent of hysterical laughter broke loose behind Jessica and Lila. Cara, Amy, Sandra, Jean and Maria were laughing so hard that they were holding onto one another for support.

Fuming with outrage, Jessica and Lila stared at their friends.

"I fail to see just what's so funny," Lila seethed, crossing her arms and breathing hard.

"Oh—oh—J-J-Jess—" Cara gasped. "Lila, you look so funny! You and your matching bikinis!" She screamed again and threw herself onto the sand.

"It's not the least *bit* funny," Jessica hissed through clenched teeth. But the sight of her friends giggling helplessly began in infect her, too, and Lila's still angry face triggered her own aughter. She began to giggle slightly, and then harder and harder as she recognized how ridiculous the situation was. Lila whirled around to glare at her, and suddenly Lila burst out laughing, too.

Soon all seven girls had tears running down their faces, and Jessica and Lila were laughing the hardest of all "Did he ask you about a million questions?" Jessica gasped, wiping a tear from her eye.

Lila nodded breathlessly. "And I thought he was so fascinated by me!"

"Me, too!"

Sandra caught her breath and pushed her short blond hair away from her face. "Boy, you guys. You really know how to pick 'em."

"Well, you have to admit," Amy put in. "He sure was gorgeous." Amy looked off in the direction in which John had disappeared, a speculative gleam in her eyes.

"Forget it, Sutton," Lila said cynically. "This is one guy you don't need."

Maria shook her head. "But don't you think he had to be pretty dense? I mean, didn't he realize all you girls would have the hots for him?"

Jessica rolled her eyes. "One thing I did discover about that guy. He's very serious about his work."

"Boy, I'll say," echoed Lila. "For a smart guy, though, he sure is dumb!"

"Now the question is, seeing as how it didn'
make a single bit of difference *what* you wrot
in your dumb ads, who won?" Cara grinned a
them mischievously, and then her look turned
to one of horror as Lila and Jessica grabbed he
arms. "No! No! I take it back!" she shrieked a
they began dragging her to the water's edge.

Screeching with laughter, the three friend
plunged into the surf and came up spluttering
and breathless. "Oh, all right!" Cara grinned a
she tossed her dripping hair out of her eyes
"You both won! Satisfied?"

The romantic strains of "Moonlight Serenade"
filled the gymnasium, and thousands of little
light sparkles reflected off a mirrored ball move
across the walls and over the couples dancing
slowly around the floor.

"You're a really good dancer, you know that?"
Neil murmured into Penny's hair.

She shrugged. "Oh, I read a book about i
once, that's all."

"You're kidding. You *are* kidding." He laughed
seeing the expression in her eyes.

"You're a real pushover, Neil." But her voic
was tender, and she nestled against him as h
steered her expertly around the dance floor.

Penny couldn't think of any day that ha
been more wonderful and dreamlike. First the
had gone to the beach concert, where they sa

together on a blanket off by themselves, enjoying the music and eating a picnic she had brought. They talked some, discovering more and more about each other; but they were often quiet, too, comfortable with an easy silence that was simply another form of communication. And now they were dancing together as if they had been doing it for years. Nothing had ever felt so right, so natural.

"I'd cut in, but I'm afraid of Neil," came a voice from behind her.

Penny looked up to see Mr. Collins smiling at them. All of a sudden she felt herself blush, and she looked shyly at Neil.

"I don't mind," Neil said politely, but with a trace of wistfulness as he let go of Penny and stepped back.

"No, no!" The English teacher chuckled. "I wouldn't dream of it. I'll see you later—for that jitterbug you promised me." With a friendly wink, he strolled off.

Elizabeth and Jeffrey revolved into their orbit. "Hi, you guys." Elizabeth smiled. "Did you go to the concert? We tried to find you, but we didn't see you anywhere."

Penny felt Neil squeeze her arm, and she repressed a grin. "Oh, we were there," she said airily, but the meaningful look she gave Elizabeth told her friend all there was to know.

Suddenly Jeffrey motioned for silence. "Hey,

Liz. Here comes Kirk. Would you say he looks kind of angry?"

Enid and her date danced into range, too, as Kirk Anderson stalked up to Elizabeth. He didn't realize it, but he had a very attentive audience.

"Liz," he said, his teeth clenched. "Where's your cousin? It's after nine o'clock! She was supposed to be here ages ago!"

A wilted corsage was crumpled in his hand, and for once, Kirk's unflinching confidence seemed to be teetering precariously on the brink.

Elizabeth looked completely mystified. "Gee, Kirk, I don't know! You mean—she isn't standing you up, is she?" She looked up swiftly at Jeffrey and then back to Kirk. "Oh, no, I had a feeling she would do this."

"What do you mean?" Kirk growled. "Do what?"

"Well, she's so awful. She's always changing her mind at the last minute and not telling anyone. Who knows, maybe she drove up and then decided she didn't want to go after all? Or maybe she just stayed in L.A. I really couldn't say. But I told you she was arrogant. I wouldn't put it past her to do anything."

Even in the dim light, it was obvious that Kirk's face had changed from ash white to beet red. With a choking snarl, he threw the crushed orchid onto the floor and stomped away.

Penny turned wondering eyes to Elizabeth.

"What was that all about, Liz? I know you don't have a cousin in New York."

She noticed Elizabeth and Enid exchange a grin, and then Elizabeth smiled at her again. "That's true, but Kirk didn't know that, did he?"

Then Jeffrey whirled her away as the music struck up again, and Penny didn't have an opportunity to ask her any more about it. Puzzled, she looked up into Neil's face. He gave her a rueful grin and shrugged. "I don't know. But I have a feeling Liz and Enid just proved how much they like you."

Penny shook her head. "If you say so. But they don't have to prove anything to me. If it wasn't for them pushing me to write that silly personal ad, we wouldn't be here tonight. I'll always be grateful for that."

"What a nasty one you are." Jeffrey chuckled in Elizabeth's ear.

"Hmm. You'd better believe it. Just stay on my good side, mister." She sighed and rested her head against Jeffrey's chest, letting the romantic music wash over them. She closed her eyes dreamily, feeling Jeffrey's strong arms holding her close. "Mmm . . . I could do this forever," she murmured.

Jeffrey's arms tightened around her. "That can be arranged," he whispered, his voice husky and deep with emotion.

Smiling blissfully, Elizabeth opened her eyes to see her sister and Lila enter the gymnasium on the arms of a pair of good-looking college boys.

Jessica spotted her and detached herself from he date to run over. Seeing her approach, Jeffrey moved off to the refreshment table. "Hi, Liz," Jessica said breathlessly.

"Is that the mysterious wonder-man?" Elizabeth asked, looking across the room at the tall, dark-haired boy her twin had come in with.

But Jessica tossed her head and snorted. "Not him! Boy, did he turn out to be a loser, but I'll tell you later. Lila and I met these guys at the beach concert—they're from Sweet Valley College. I did OK, huh? Even without a personal ad."

"Oh, Jessica! You don't need anything but your own self to meet boys, you maniac!"

"What are you two blabbing about?" Jeffrey cut in, handing Elizabeth a cup of punch and taking a sip of his own.

Jessica gave him an arch smile. "Oh, nothing. But isn't it funny how things have a way of working out?"

As Penny and Neil floated by, lost in their own world, Elizabeth felt herself grinning. Across the room Kirk Anderson was sulking by the locker-room doors, scowling at everyone who danced by. "You're right, Jess. It sure is."

A few minutes later, Jessica grabbed Lila by

the arm and dragged her to the restroom. "Come on."

"OK, OK!" Lila said, prying Jessica's fingers from her arm. "What's got into you?"

Jessica cast a quick look about her. "I have this funny feeling," she mumbled.

Pushing open the bathroom door, the two girls hurried inside. But just as Jessica was about to speak, they realized they weren't alone.

Regina Morrow turned away from the mirror, her hairbrush poised. "Hi."

"Regina!" Jessica exclaimed. The lovely dark-haired girl smiled back at them, but Jessica thought she detected a look of worry in Regina's dark eyes.

"I didn't know you were here tonight," said Lila. "I didn't see Bruce anywhere."

A fleeting frown passed over Regina's forehead. "Oh, he decided at the last minute he had too much work to do, so I came alone just for fun."

Lila's eyes opened wide. "We're talking about the same Bruce Patman, aren't we? He's staying home to do schoolwork on a Saturday night?"

Nonchalantly stepping up to the mirror, Jessica opened her makeup bag and began applying a coat of lip gloss. "What's he working on, do you know?"

"Some oral report he's been really wrapped up in," Regina answered hesitantly.

"Isn't that nice." Jessica kept her eyes fixed

on her own reflection, but her mind was rapidly going over the students she had seen in the gym just minutes before. Was Amy Sutton there? She had been with them at the beach, but now that Jessica thought about it, she couldn't remember seeing Amy at the dance. What she had been planning to tell Lila about was now a certainty, as far as Jessica was concerned. Could Amy's plan to snare Bruce actually be working?

Her glance slid over to Regina, who was absently brushing her long, glossy hair. Born almost totally deaf, Regina had committed her life to overcoming the handicap. When she had moved to Sweet Valley, most people didn't even realize she couldn't hear. Her courage and determination had impressed everybody, as had her elegant beauty and poise.

At first when arrogant, spoiled Bruce Patman had fallen in love with her, and she with him, everyone had been surprised. But Regina's influence had turned Bruce into a caring person, and nobody could have been happier than he was when a series of treatments in Switzerland had restored Regina's hearing completely. So it seemed impossible that he could lose interest in the sensitive girl who loved him.

But with a determined Amy Sutton scheming to get Bruce, perhaps that was just what was happening.

*Will Amy succeed in luring
Bruce away from Regina? Find
out in Sweet Valley High #40,*
ON THE EDGE.